IN THE TANK—A BOUND BLOG

IN THE TANK—A BOUND BLOG

How the Media Political Machine Used Conveyance of Toxic Information to Become the Latest Political Force to Be Reckoned With

BY

MARK A. ANDERSON

iUniverse, Inc.
New York   Bloomington

In the Tank—A Bound Blog
How the Media Political Machine Used Conveyance of Toxic
Information to Become the Latest Political Force to Be Reckoned With

iUniverse books may be ordered through booksellers or by contacting:

iUniverse
1663 Liberty Drive
Bloomington, IN 47403
www.iuniverse.com
1-800-Authors (1-800-288-4677)

ISBN: 978-1-4401-6281-7 (sc)
ISBN: 978-1-4401-6282-4 (ebook)
ISBN: 978-1-4401-6283-1 (dj)

Printed in the United States of America

iUniverse Rev. 10/29/09

I dedicate this book to my beloved parents, and to my beautiful wife who served as my inspiration for this work.

"Media have tremendous power in setting cultural guidelines and in shaping political discourse. It is essential that the news media, along with other institutions, are challenged to be fair and accurate. The first step in challenging biased news coverage is documenting bias."—Fairness and Accuracy In Reporting (FAIR)

FAIR is a national media watchdog group that has offered extensive documented criticism of media bias and censorship since 1986.

PROLOGUE

In recent times, the integrity of the news media, in various forms, has been compromised by the corrupting influences of network owners, major sponsoring interests, and off center leaning journalists and correspondents who seem more interested in influencing viewers' thoughts than maintaining the dignity of their craft. Although it is not clear when the practice of self interest driven bias entered the equation of day to day news reporting, when it first became noticeable to most is when the FOX News network commandeered the reins of news mass media and began reporting all things newsworthy with a right leaning spin while in the same breath referring to itself as both "fair and balanced." In turn, the popularity of intellectually stimulating news programs such as "60 Minutes," "20/20," and "Meet the Press," began to dwindle in favor of Ringling Brothers, Barnum and Bailey styled news reporting that was far more entertaining, opinionated, and negative in nature.

When I was much younger, I remember being confused by this manner of reporting, and watching my father angrily change the television channel to another news station—any news station other than FOX. As an adult, I too became angered when I finally realized that the manner of news reporting employed by FOX was nothing more than an effort to rob me of my opinions, independent thoughts, and, most recently, my vote, by whomever controlled the media outlet from which I obtained tainted newsworthy information. To put it simply, one would not purchase goods from a store if the contents had been tampered with or had the safety seals broken on them, because this is an indication that the goods could be defective and prove to be harmful to the consumer. More importantly, the absence of any form of seal on the product is an indication that the guarantee of freshness and safety from the manufacturer is null and void. I began to wonder why I should accept any less of a guarantee from a news media outlet that served as the conduit between myself and the origin of a given news story. Instead of acting as an honest broker, much as my local discount retailer, by passing the goods on to the consumer in the same sealed manner it was received from the manufacturer, now the mainstream news media was, instead, breaking the seals on the goods, adding toxic ingredients of their choosing to the contents, then passing it on to the consumer, in this case the program viewer.

After watching broadcast upon broadcast of my favorite news programs during the Republican and Democratic Primary elections of 2008, it became readily apparent to me that something had gone seriously awry. I was shocked to find the bias that was now so common in daily news media broadcasts was even more pronounced at such a critical period in the history of our nation's elections for the highest elected office in the land. At first, I felt that maybe I was reading too deeply into what it was the news correspondents were saying and what various news media journalists wrote at the time, and further, that I was hearing and seeing shameless bias that was not really there, or was at least not as extreme as I perceived. I then asked my wife, who preferred watching comedy shows and the latest in a series of reality shows featuring some guy in search of true love, rather than the latest "breaking news," to watch some of the news broadcasts with me during the time of the 2008 primary elections. At the conclusion of the broadcasts, without attempting to cloud her judgment with my own opinions or bombarding her with leading questions, I simply asked her how she felt about what she saw and heard. She promptly confirmed my suspicion with one simple all encompassing phrase. "Animal Farm," she said, referring to the grade school classic book by George Orwell in which satirical character Napoleon, the gruff and strong willed Berkshire boar, used iron fisted governing techniques and self serving propaganda and rhetoric to control the animals living on a farm they liberated from its human occupants. The relationship between the American news media and its consumers was beginning to have a strange likeness to that between the animal society on *Animal Farm*, Napoleon, a totalitarian type leader, and Squealer, his official spokesperson or press secretary. The leaders of Orwell's satirical animal society started out on a somewhat even plane as representatives of the animals they led. It was soon realized by the leaders on the farm, however, that they had the complete trust of the others and the spoken word was the most powerful tool at their disposal. As a result of this, the interest of all citizens of their largely four legged society quickly gave way to the interest of the few, those in power and positions of influence, as well as the members of the leaders' elite inner circle. The forms of propaganda and rhetoric used in Orwell's *Animal Farm* have been openly denounced by Western nations and identified as being a method of control frequently used by communist and other non-democratic nations to malevolently mold the minds of its citizenry and cripple any effort for them to maintain freedom of thought. Ironically, this was and is the same form of propaganda being so freely used by the American news media to disenfranchise viewers by aggressively shepherding them through the broad gateways of a herd mentality like the slogan bleating sheep in Orwell's book. It soon became apparent to me that in 2008 virtually all major national news television networks, as well as countless news publication entities, had adopted the practice of injecting an off-center spin into virtually everything they provided coverage on. This tainted coverage included, but was not limited to issues regarding the environment, the war in Iraq, and coverage of the 2008 elections for the presidency of the United States, rendering all toxic in nature, in an effort to influence the thinking of the American populace as well as to influence the outcome of both the party primaries and the General Election.

So what exactly *is* this toxic news reporting of which I speak? Well, if news reporting in its pure and unadulterated form is defined as the conveyance of factual newsworthy information of a local, national, or global level to parties interested, then toxic news reporting is that which encroaches upon the integrity or unbent truthfulness of this information in a manner that compels it to be transformed into what is more opinion of the conveyor than actual fact. The danger of toxic news reporting lies with the detrimental effects it has on the thoughts and views of the receiver, who then forms opinions based on the information received from a "trusted" news media source or agent, who uses the conveyance of this information to persuade or mislead. This process, in turn, often leads to actions being taken by the receiver of the information based on these toxic opinions. These actions can be as minor as siding with one political party over another regarding its ideology on a given issue, or as major as preference for one candidate for public office over another based on overly positive or favorable information conveyed by the news media regarding one candidate versus mostly negative information conveyed regarding another candidate, both of which may include information that is not entirely factual. Whatever the case may be, when the news media abuses its responsibility as the trusted conveyor of newsworthy facts and instead engages in the act of conveying biased opinions disguised as facts to its viewers, this can be referred to as toxic news reporting.

Politically charged spin or toxicity in news reporting, once most commonly found at the FOX News network as well as with its affiliate news outlets, consisting of one third serious journalism and two thirds entertainment and spin, with time, became accepted as normal for that particular network. Now, however, not only are other serious and "trusted" networks engaging in rhetorically charged and heavily biased news reporting, but they are, arguably, even more biased and extreme in the methods of reporting they employ to influence the political beliefs and opinions of their viewers—even more so than the FOX News network. By the time of the 2008 presidential elections, toxic news reporting had made its way through the ranks of leading news media outlets like an infectious disease, and there was no end to its reign in sight. This fact became most apparent after the American news media successfully decimated the Hillary Clinton campaign bid for the presidency during the Democratic Party primary elections through the use of overtly toxic and negative spin while providing coverage of her political campaign. This victory over the so called "Clinton Political Machine" signified both the end of an era of Democratic Party politics largely dominated by the Clintons as well as the emergence of possibly the largest most powerful, corruptible, and influential force in the future of American politics—the Media Political Machine. By successfully reducing the vast and lifelong public service record of arguably one of the most influential women in the world to merely being the overly ambitious wife of an "increasingly irrelevant" former President, and by overtly bolstering the somewhat shorter public service record of another through overwhelmingly positive press coverage of both he and his campaign, the news media emerged as the uncontested victor in the race for the Democratic Party nomination for President in 2008 and had its eyes set on influencing the outcome of the General Election. Its strength had been tested, never faltering, as the concerted effort of its many networks and publications proved to the world that the control and conveyance of information ruled the nation, no matter what impure and sullied form it came in.

Some may ask the question, where is the truth in this observation when the nation's media, more specifically, news media, is so often referred to as the "liberal media?" The truth of the matter is one would only have to watch five minutes of FOX News, read the latest carefully selected headlines of the Drudge Report, or have witnessed the way CNN, MSNBC, and *Newsweek* among other media outlets, took a wrecking ball to the Hillary Clinton campaign for the presidency in 2008 to realize the news media is by no means a yellow dog, left wing serving entity. The label "liberal media" is in all actuality a misnomer most likely thought up by some conservative political strategist seeking to dupe the news media into lightening its coverage of blunders and missteps often made by Republican Party standard bearers and elected officials. No. If the news media of this nation ever was a politically left leaning entity, it is definitely no longer. In recent years, as a collective, the so called "liberal media" spent more time scrutinizing and questioning the every move of former President Bill Clinton than reporting facts, in the spirit of accountability, about President George W. Bush's ever failing attempt at doing anything that would raise his anemic public approval rating. The fact of the matter is, the media is no more liberal than it is conservative and is instead a self serving entity that rents itself out to the highest bidder, he who has done something for it lately, or he who can possibly do something for it in the future such as bring it awards, praise, accolades, and even increased revenue for the most coverage of a historical political event of a monumental nature.

INTRODUCTION

The primaries and General Election of 2008 will go down in our nation's history as one of the most exciting and eventful national election seasons ever. The world was introduced to one of the most electrifying and articulate politicians of modern history who rose from the status of Washington newcomer and political underdog to emerge as one of the most promising Democratic Party nominees for the presidency since longtime Arkansas Governor, William Jefferson Clinton. Our nation was re-introduced to one of the most intelligent, influential, and respected women in the world who rose above all odds to run a campaign for her party's nomination with the drive and dedication of one hundred male candidates combined, inspiring women everywhere to never doubt themselves or their potential for success and greatness again. We also witnessed the re-birth of a political phoenix from the state of Arizona who emerged from the ashes of previous national political defeat as one of America's most seasoned and experienced party nominees for the presidency since Ronald Wilson Reagan, regarded as a maverick to some, but respected by all. The political playing field of the 2008 election season was filled with some of the absolute best politicians to ever grace the halls of our nation's state and national government institutions, from former governors to serving senators to an enigmatic physician turned congressman from Texas, and a congressman from Ohio with the courage and integrity to introduce articles of impeachment against a sitting Vice President. Though Americans and the world alike had a chance to witness our wonderful democracy at its very best during the year's election season, both were also subjected to the worst we had to offer in regards to news media coverage of the primary elections and the days leading up to the General Election of the 44th President of the United States of America.

While citizens of our great nation watched from the sidelines as our intricate election process was set in motion to select the latest leader of the free world, and while our best and most qualified leaders of American politics argued their case for the position to concerned citizens of all nations, a political campaign of another more clandestine nature was being conducted right under our very noses. This was a campaign not sanctioned by the Republicans, Democrats, Independents, or even the Green Party. It also was not a campaign conducted by any other interest group seeking deviation from the norm of the framework of our free election system. It was instead a campaign of a more wily and covert nature that was so complex, widespread, and synchronized that initially one would have to take a second look to notice its very existence. This campaign was waged not only against individual candidates, campaigns, their respective political parties, and varying ideologies, but also against the unsuspecting citizens and voters of America seeking only to make an informed and conscious decision as to who would be the best person to fill a position that was so badly in need of a new sense of direction. It was moreover waged against the very foundation of our nation, our collective political ideals, and the democratic way of life we have fought so hard both to preserve and introduce to those who have never known it—specifically freedom and the freedom to choose.

Using some of the most underhanded and malicious tactics ever seen in the history of our nation's political system, the trusted custodians of the airwaves and presses, the American news media, successfully launched and conducted a political campaign of its own, that injected spin and bias in its most toxic form, into the delivery of almost every story related to the 2008 elections in pursuit of the presidency. In addition to this, the news media took it upon itself to attempt to make decisions for American voters regarding whom to support during the caucuses and primaries, as well as the General Election, through the conveying of contaminated information passed off as raw and uncut facts. Regular practices of the largest and most influential appendages of the news media during the 2008 election campaign season included the overt support of one candidate over all others, the unrelenting demonizing of other candidates which bordered on gender discrimination, the discrimination against the age of yet another candidate, and the total dismissal of the existence of all other candidates even while they were yet contenders for their respective party's presidential nomination. Some of the most malevolent tactics employed by the news media during the elections included conducting unverifiable independent polls, posing news media correspondents as subject matter experts regarding intricate political issues, supporting positions of self-interest with biased panels, and the outright use of unprofessional and disrespectful language when referring to or speaking about select individuals involved in the 2008 presidential election and campaign process, to include candidates. What was worse was the fact that the news media attempted its takeover of the American democratic election process at a time when it was most critical to elect an informed, qualified, and skilled leader ready to counter eight years of failed policies, a sagging economy, as well as a war that American society was growing wearier of by the day.

Because nobody spoke out against the offenses of unfettered bias spewed by leading news media outlets during election season '08, save for the occasional private citizen and political blogger fed up with being overwhelmed with more opinion than verifiable fact, the news media became empowered and even bolder in its toxic reporting activities with each passing day. Politicians who benefited from the news media's lack of balance refused to speak out when others were attacked unfairly by news journalists and correspondents, and politicians who spoke out against news media attacks on them were met with even more negative press from the news media who insisted that it was performing its duties in the most fair, balanced, and trusted manner possible, free from both "bias" or "bull." Leading news media networks, magazines, and Websites refused to discipline writers and correspondents who crossed the line of objectivity and professionalism even during live broadcasts, while instead choosing to reward the news media's most frequent biased offenders with lead roles throughout the media world which, ironically, gave them increased autonomy to perform their duties in an even more toxic manner than before. All occurred at the expense of American society and voters who sought only to be informed of newsworthy facts and social issues effecting their lives, to allow for them to make informed decisions when assessing the issues and the candidates associated with one of the most important General Elections in modern American history. Instead of facilitating this process through the simple task of performing its duties in a manner that benefited the very people who depended upon it to act on their behalf and report the details of various issues in an unprejudiced manner, the American news media took it upon itself to disregard the need for conveyance of facts to American society in favor of benefiting itself through injecting toxicity into all facets of news reporting having anything to do with the most current election process.

The same news media that prided itself with bringing the wrongs committed by various individuals and institutions onto the world stage for all to see during the most critical periods in our nation's history to include the Civil Rights Movement, the assassination of President John F. Kennedy, the Vietnam War, and the days following the attacks of September 11, had compromised its integrity, sold its soul for political and financial gain, and could no longer be trusted. So, who will the people turn to now? Who will keep them informed of wrongs committed by society against minorities, the downtrodden, and less fortunate of this great nation? Who will report the facts about the activities of politicians no matter how powerful or popular they are? Who will accurately report the situation on the ground in countries that are growing more and more unstable by the day despite the presence of the Armed Forces of the most powerful nation on earth? Who will be the voice of the fallen as it relates to the same? The news media of Cronkite, Jennings, Shaw, and Brokaw has evolved into a grotesque mutation of itself and is growing more powerful and moving farther off course with each biohazard laden broadcast aired and article written, as well as with each convert that joins its swollen ranks.

The following literary work consists of my personal documentation of some of the most extreme and blatant cases of toxic news reporting employed, during election season 2008, by many of the most powerful and prominent news media outlets known to American society, as proof of its often denied occurrence. In addition to this, I also present the most effective tactics of toxic news reporting, exhibited during the 2008 elections, that were so commonly used that they could not be ignored or denied and left no question as to the clandestine motives of the Media Political Machine. These motives of which I speak included, among other things, the attempt to determine the outcome of the 2008 General Election whether it was the actual will of the people or not. These tactics were employed copiously by the American news media during the '08 campaign season and are well documented throughout, serving as further evidence of the existence of a covert political campaign conducted by the American news media that served to impede the momentum and success of legitimate political campaigns that ran counter to its choice for the 44th President of the United States. Ranging from brazenly overt to barely detectible in nature, these tactics of ill intent, employed by the news media, were plentiful during the most recent election season and were skillfully used to influence viewers and voters regarding issues and individuals involved in national election process.

Being both a bit of a history and political science buff, as a direct result of my earning both undergraduate and graduate degrees in the fields, respectively, I possess an acute interest in the progress of our nation's society as well as in its rich, though often less than noble history. As a soldier who served during a critical period in the defense of this nation and its citizens, as well as in the capacity of a Casualty Assistance Officer for a fallen soldier who was also a dear friend, I understand the importance of waging war as an absolute last result, and the virtues of quality leadership during challenging times. It is imperative that we maintain and protect our nation's free election system so that it always remains the true will and voice of the people, and is never allowed to become controlled by those who have the interest of only the wealthy, powerful, prominent, or the few at heart. This is by no means an attempt to turn readers or viewers of these media outlets against them or away from news reporting and journalism in its purest form, but is instead a chronological account of the failure of these outlets and news providers to protect the interest of viewers and subscribers who once had trust in them to provide newsworthy, unaffected, factual information which allows for independent thought and the freedom to decide as is an extension of our inalienable rights as citizens of this free nation.

25 March 2008

Numerous news media stations spent the majority of the evening discussing how Senator Hillary Clinton "misspoke" regarding the issue of dodging sniper fire during a trip to Bosnia, a claim she made several times during the early days of the Democratic primary elections. The coverage the news media afforded the story amounted to overkill which sent multiple negative messages to program viewers and voters regarding Clinton's credibility. The CNN Website, under its Election Center 2008 section, vigorously contested Clinton's claim with thoroughly researched evidence to the contrary. One line in the story titled "Clinton says she 'misspoke' about sniper fire,"[1] regarding the controversial subject stated, "but news footage of her arrival at Tuzla shows Clinton, then the first lady, calmly walking from the rear ramp of a U.S. Air Force plane with her daughter, Chelsea, then 16, at her side."[2] The Website also published a statement in the same story, issued by a spokesperson for the Obama campaign, stating Clinton's claim was part of "a growing list of instances in which Sen. Clinton has exaggerated her role in foreign and domestic policymaking."[3] It was obvious the author of the story sought to inject as much negativity as was possible at the time regarding Clinton's account of what happened on the day in question. The writer skillfully used the statement issued by the Obama campaign in the lines of the story to add to the negative effect. There was no effort evident on this evening, or those following soon thereafter, to downplay the story in any manner and help Clinton get past the controversy that was having an obvious detrimental impact on her campaign efforts at the time. On the contrary, the news media, in both broadcast and print form, seemed to add to Clinton's woes through a concerted effort to amplify the controversy and admonish her for making such a claim. During the same time period, in sharp contrast, media correspondents and networks, when speaking about Senator Barack Obama portrayed and described him as a devoted family man as he spent the Easter holiday in the Virgin Islands with his wife and children.

CNN, on the same night, reported a story about Chelsea Clinton fielding a question from a member of an audience gathered to hear her speak regarding her mother's candidacy for the presidency. The quite inappropriate question fielded to her had to do with the effects of the Monica Lewinski scandal on Senator Clinton while she was yet the First Lady. Chelsea quickly replied that out of over seventy college campuses visited and hundreds of questions asked, this was the first one fielded to her of its nature, and was further nobody's business due to the personal nature of the issue. Several news correspondents and networks that covered the story made it a point to discuss Chelsea's response as if she should not have responded in such a manner and should have given more insight into the Clintons' personal family affairs.

07 April 2008

Former President Bill and Hillary Clinton's financial earnings were heavily scrutinized by multiple news media networks after their tax returns for the year prior were released during the Democratic and Republican Party primary elections, revealing a combined income in excess of one hundred million dollars. Though it was pointed out that the bulk of their earnings came from the former President's book sales and numerous speaking engagements, their finances were scrutinized by several news media television networks because they made sizable donations to the charitable organization they founded. The same networks gave an honorable mention to Senator Barack Obama regarding his income combined with that of his wife Michelle for the same year, however it was apparent that the news media was most obsessed with the sizeable earnings of the Clintons. It seemed as if the release of these tax records touched off a media firestorm fueled by jealousy and sentiments that the Clintons made far more money than they should have as was made evident by extensive discussion devoted to the subject on several news media networks. The million dollar question was—by whose standard? I wondered about the relevance of the issue to the race for the Democratic Party nomination.

11 April 2008

MSNBC broke a story regarding a statement made by Senator Obama at a campaign rally in Pennsylvania during which he referred to some Pennsylvanians as being "bitter" due to their deteriorating economic status, resulting in their clinging to "guns and religion." The comments were reportedly not well received by citizens of the state, however the daytime correspondent who covered the story in the days following, interviewed several seemingly pro-Obama guests which she asked, on several occasions, if the media was "making too much" of the story and fueling debate regarding what it was that Obama actually meant when he made the statements. This reeked of an attempt to persuade viewers to give Obama a pass regarding statements that some viewed as elitist and left him seeming out of touch with the American public. When Democratic presidential hopeful Senator Hillary Clinton commented on the political misstep made by Obama in Pennsylvania in the days following, MSNBC correspondents criticized Clinton's attempt to capitalize on the issue, saying she was "taking things too far" by speaking out regarding the controversy. One member of a panel assembled by the network commented that Senator Clinton should not have made statements regarding Obama's verbal misstep as sounding elitist when she and former President Clinton raked in over one hundred million dollars worth of income in 2007. The reference to the Clinton's income was sorely irrelevant to the subject at hand yet was still entertained by the daytime correspondent reporting on the Obama story. In addition to this, the panel member who gave several indications during the program of being an Obama supporter seemed angered at the news of the Clintons' amount of reported income for the previous year almost as if they had no right to earn such an impressive amount.

MSNBC News Website section entitled "Decision '08" displayed a story it referred to as one of its "Top Political Stories," titled "Now Bill Makes a Bosnia Blooper"[4] which consisted of two empty and obviously one-sided commentaries by Chuck Todd, the network's

Political Director, and Mark Murray, the network's Deputy Political Director. The story read as a rehash of Hillary Clinton's Bosnia sniper fire verbal slip up, only this time the former President was pulled into the mix as he attempted to run damage control for her regarding the potentially politically detrimental issue. The commentary mocked him as the nation's "increasingly irrelevant" former President and an albatross to Hillary's campaign for the presidency. Both commentary pieces were nonsensically lopsided and showed no signs of balance or contrast. It seemed that it was another overt attempt by representatives of the news media, this time fairly high ranking, to heap negativity on candidate Hillary Clinton and the Clinton legacy during the primary campaign season in efforts to turn American voters completely against her and the former President.

Another story featured on the MSNBC news Website that day was titled "Why Clinton Is Fighting So Hard"[5] by Eleanor Clift. The story was published by *Newsweek* magazine. This commentary focused yet again on former President Clinton campaigning for Senator Clinton because he was said to be "afraid" his legacy would somehow be lessened in significance if Senator Obama was elected as the "first black President of the United States." The story was sharply biased against both Clintons and highly negative language was used throughout the piece to describe the reasoning behind the former President's efforts to support his *wife* on the campaign trail. "The former president is working harder on the road to get Hillary elected than he did in 1996 to get himself re-elected, judging by the jam-packed schedule of 'Solutions for America' events staged in school gymnasiums from morning until night in all corners of the two states. Except for an occasional red-faced outburst over a media slight or someone's perceived disloyalty, he's soldiering away with extraordinary discipline,"[6] Clift wrote scathingly. In the highly biased story, Clift also boldly made the claim regarding the former President that he was, "also doing penance for how much he humiliated her when he was president, and even for some of his missteps in this campaign, mostly having to do with race. But perhaps most important, Clinton understands that if Barack Obama is elected, his presidency becomes an asterisk."[7] The story never fully explained why exactly the former President's tenure as the nation's

Chief Executive would become an "asterisk" following an Obama General Election victory. After all, the pages of history regarding the Clinton presidency had already been written and the former President had not been caught using performance enhancing drugs during his time in office. The commentary curiously went on to talk about all the power Senator Obama would have at his disposal, if elected, with the potential for a majority in the U.S. Senate close to sixty seats and fifteen additional in the U.S. House of Representatives following the election, which would have been a case in point if the same would not have been true if Senator Clinton won the Democratic nomination for the presidency and went on to win the General Election instead. The opposite scenario, highlighting Senator Clinton's potential for a presidency with a Democratic majority in the House and Senate was opportunely not argued. The commentary did, however, discuss at length what Senator Clinton's legacy would be if she indeed *lost* the Democratic Party nomination to Senator Obama, as if making its early prediction. The commentary ended by suggestively stating how "a fresh start" would be more effective against John McCain in the General Election, insinuating voters should support Senator Obama in the Democratic primaries because he was touted as being a Washington outsider as well as an advocate for "change."[8] No reference was made in the story regarding Senator Clinton's arguable advantage over Obama in regards to overall leadership experience, nor in regards to being a just as formidable opponent for Senator McCain in the General Election. Clift refrained from making any points in the story for the sake of balance or objectivity which made it read like a hit piece on the Clintons for purpose of rendering Senator Obama a more appealing candidate for the Democratic Party nomination.

25 April 2008

Former CNN White House Correspondent John King covered a story on the evening's broadcast of "Anderson Cooper 360," focusing on the violent crime wave involving African American youth in the city of Chicago.[9] Though the story featured a Chicago law enforcement officer who recently lost his own son to an act of violence in the city, the story was prefaced with footage of none other than Senator Barack

Obama speaking to a group regarding what should be done and what steps should be taken to curb the violence. A video clip was played with Obama making the following statements: "A lot of emphasis is going to be put on more effective community policing. A lot of emphasis is going to be put on how we are working together to give young people more constructive things to do and give to give them more perspective in terms of why violence is unacceptable."[10] CNN Correspondent King followed up the video clip with the statement: "Senator Barack Obama talking earlier today about how to stop the wave of violence sweeping his home city of Chicago. Senator Obama told reporters he plans to meet with school officials to discuss this crisis."[11] This cleverly equated to more positive press time for Senator Obama. No such air time, of a similar nature, was afforded to candidates Hillary Clinton or Republican presumptive nominee John McCain, however, in addition to this story, the network aired a story during which South Carolina Representative James Clyburn commented negatively regarding remarks made by former President Bill Clinton, that the Obama campaign was playing the race card during the campaign. An audio clip of Clinton stating the following was played: "I think that they played the race card on me. And we now know, from memos from the campaign and everything, that they planned to do it all along." Clyburn critically referred to the former President's words as "bizarre"[12] in nature and said that he could not believe Clinton would make such an accusation. Dialogue ensued regarding the issue, facilitated by network correspondents calling for former President Clinton to stay out of the campaign spotlight. CNN Correspondent Jessica Yellin also added during the broadcast that a *fact check* yielded that the claim made by former President Clinton that the Obama campaign had memos citing the intent to use the race card against him during the campaign season as unfounded. Terms were then used in reference to the actions former President Clinton should take during the remainder of the elections that were highly disrespectful, especially when referring to one of the nation's former Chief Executives. This form of talk was noticeably unprecedented and unlike any dialogue used on television news networks in reference to other former Presidents of the United States. Additional negativity was heaped on the both Clintons during the evening network broadcast when John King asked guest and longtime Hillary Clinton supporter, Congresswoman Stephanie Tubbs Jones to respond to a statement, attributed to Congressman Clyburn. The manner in which King presented the statement as a lead in to the guest appearance by Tubbs Jones, a Hillary Clinton supporter, was easily identifiable as both highly toxic and leading in nature. "Congresswoman Tubbs Jones, I want to begin with you, because Congressman Clyburn has a pretty loaded charge. He says the Clintons, plural, and especially Bill Clinton, will do all they can to destroy Barack Obama to the point he can't win a general election. That's a pretty tough charge,"[13] said King. Though Tubbs Jones skillfully negotiated the toxic minefield laid by one of CNN's lead correspondents during the election season, dismissing the charge as baseless, King succeeded in planting more seeds of doubt and negativity during a primetime news broadcast that arguably cost the Clinton campaign much credibility in the days to come.

All of this toxic reporting followed on the heels of a primary election win for Senator Clinton in the state of Pennsylvania where she defeated Senator Obama by a margin of ten percentage points. Little coverage or reflection was made regarding Clinton's victory, instead another "independent poll" was unveiled in which voters were asked who they supported as the Democratic Party nominee. It was conducted in Indiana due to the state being the site of one of the next Democratic primary elections. The result was reported as 45% for Clinton, and 45% for Obama with 10% of those poll remaining undecided, reflecting the two candidates in a dead heat for the upcoming state primary. On an evening that should have yielded at least some positive coverage for Clinton, citing her victory in a major primary election, leading news media correspondents found reasons to heap negativity upon both the Senator and the former President, turning it into a night of praise for Senator Obama.

29 April 2008

One day after Reverend Jeremiah Wright, Senator Obama's pastor of over twenty years who married him to his wife Michelle and baptized his two young daughters, delivered a controversial fire and brimstone address to an annual NAACP function, declaring himself a minister and not a politician and taking critics of himself and the African American church to task regarding "differences" in white America and the rest of the nation's citizens, Senator Obama decisively distanced himself from his former pastor by publicly stating he was both offended and hurt by the strong words of Wright and assured the voting public that his relationship with Wright had changed as a result and that Reverend Wright spoke for neither him or his campaign.

On MSNBC's Hardball with Chris Matthews, several of the network's correspondents as well as guest, New Mexico Governor Bill Richardson, offered praise for Senator Obama for openly distancing himself from Reverend Wright and denouncing Wright's actions as both selfish and hate filled, which some viewed as Obama denouncing his African American heritage to appease white voters who were clearly offended by Wright's speech to the NAACP. Curiously, Wright's speech made no case for hatred as MSNBC correspondents suggested, nor did make mention of the rejection of any race, but instead forcefully highlighted the historical tendencies of *some* (not all) whites to view themselves as of a superior race to all others of this nation and the world. Though Senator Obama clearly had a more than casual relationship with Reverend Wright, as evidenced by his endorsement of Wright's religious ideology through attending the church Wright pastored for over twenty years, agents of the American news media performed emergency damage control operations for Senator Obama through an interview with Governor Richardson who applauded Obama's denouncing Reverend Wright and resurrecting, with the help of correspondent Chris Matthews, the issue of Richardson being compared to Judas when he endorsed Senator Obama instead of Senator Clinton despite a longtime close relationship with she and the former President. In his interview, Richardson cited what he described as the Clintons' perceived thinking that they were entitled to the Presidency through divine right, despite this point never surfacing from he or any other political leader or news media correspondent when President George W. Bush was elected to the presidency following in the footsteps of his own father who served as President prior to Bill Clinton. Matthews initiated a toxic dialogue with Richardson in regards to his view with the following statements. "Why do you think the Clinton's have been so tough on you, saying that you promised them all those times to not back Barack Obama? Why are they so vengeful towards you?"[14] Richardson replied on cue, by stating, "Well I regret it very much, because I still have a lot of affection for them. But you know, I've always said, there's a certain view that they're entitled to the presidency that they've had. And anybody that deviated from that, I believe, you know, is going to be the subject of their scorn."[15] Neither Matthews nor Richardson provided facts supporting this claim against the Clintons, however it seemed as if this idea of divine right was mentioned to plant the seeds of hate and discontent in the minds of voters regarding the idea of a possible second Clinton presidency.

Around the same time Governor Richardson was being compared to Judas for his support of Senator Obama, which the news media portrayed as both undeserved and wrong, Senator Obama openly denounced his pastor of twenty years following Wright's controversial speech before the NAACP. This though Senator Obama had, in the past, referred to Reverend Wright as "like an uncle" to him and a trusted spiritual advisor. During this period of controversy for Obama, multiple news networks awarded him a pass and heaped pity upon him, even characterizing him as "genuinely hurt" by Wright's speech to the NAACP and to the comments he made in response to questions asked of him at a National Press Club gathering, as if they could see directly into the Senator's heart.

On the same day, little mention was made of a key superdelegate endorsement for Senator Clinton by the Governor of North Carolina. MSNBC and other news media outlets chose instead to hone in on the Governor's choice of words used during his endorsement speech. The governor commented that Senator Clinton's resilience during the campaign made Rocky Balboa look like a "pansy." News media correspondents reporting the story quickly injected their own toxicity and spin, attempting to turn a story that should have been positive for Senator Clinton, especially on the heels of the Reverend Jeremiah Wright controversy, into something negative by focusing on the governor's word choice instead of on his reasoning for his endorsement of Clinton. By the end of the story, in its toxic form, viewers who did not hear the Governor's remarks verbatim were left with the sense that he was actually referring to Senator Obama as a pansy when this was clearly not the case.

30 April 2008

CNN White House correspondent and former Bush Administration sympathizer, Suzanne Malveaux, interviewed Michelle Obama with Caroline Kennedy at her side to continue the media driven damage control effort to minimize the fallout resulting from Reverend Jeremiah Wright's speech and comments to the National Press Club. Prior to this however, a CNN first, "behind the scenes" look was given to viewers by correspondent Erica Hill featuring Senator Clinton going to a gas station to speak to "average Americans" regarding the pain caused at the pump by ever increasing fuel prices. It was pointed out by Hill that the "average Joe" Clinton was seen with at the gas station in one clip of footage was "chosen" by the Clinton campaign because he fit the profile that the campaign was looking for in the photo op. Clinton was also shown at the counter inside the small gas station, set up by the filming crew and campaign, seemingly surprised to see individuals standing behind her that she had not noticed before when in fact the whole thing was staged for maximum effect. Seeing the behind the scenes stagecraft particulars left me with wondering if Senator Clinton was genuine with her concern for gas pump woes or simply performing for the audience which was undoubtedly the desired effect. No such behind the scenes look at stagecraft was given that evening for the Barack Obama campaign.

Following the behind the scenes stagecraft piece, CNN featured a brief, yet impressive biography of Michelle Obama highlighting her education and her most prominent life changing event— meeting Barack Obama. On the heels of such coverage of the Obamas, Larry King, on the evening broadcast of Larry King Live, featured controversial filmmaker Michael Moore. King prefaced the broadcast by informing viewers that Moore had recently endorsed Senator Obama for the Democratic Party nomination. Just prior to the airing of King's program, however, a brief look was given to the Democratic Party delegate and superdelegate totals for Senators Obama and Clinton respectively. It was pointed out that Clinton had an "uphill battle" to win enough support to find favor with undecided delegates and superdelegates to clinch the Democratic Party nomination. When Larry King Live aired, Michael Moore elaborated on his reasons for supporting Barack Obama for the Democratic nomination. Moore openly praised Senator Obama yet criticized the Clinton campaign for fueling the controversy surrounding Reverend Jeremiah Wright. During the interview, Moore stated regarding Obama: "As far as a candidate, I think that this is a very decent individual. And I've been just impressed through the various debates as to how he's handled himself, how he has responded to the issues and responded to people."[16] Larry King then cited harsh words used by Michael Moore referring to his disgust for Senator Clinton, even stating that she was "smearing the black man" (Senator Obama) in a campaign that she "could not win." During the interview, King quoted Moore regarding the recent pointed statements that Moore made about Clinton. "Over the past few months, the actions and words of Hillary Clinton have gone from being merely disappointing to downright disgusting,"[17] King quoted Moore as saying. King also quoted statements that Moore was said to have written to Clinton directly during the campaign season. "You have devoted your life to good causes and good deeds. And now to throw it all away for an office you can't win unless you smear the black man so much that the superdelegates cry Uncle Tom and give it all to you,"[18] Moore wrote. During the remainder of the interview, the manner in which Moore described Clinton and Obama displayed a very sharp contrast that bordered on fanaticism for Obama and utter contempt for Clinton. Larry King made no attempt to introduce objectivity into the broadcast, instead allowing Moore to stump for Obama during the live broadcast while railing against Clinton. For the remainder of the interview, Moore went on to speak candidly regarding his opinion on several politically charged subjects which led to yet more cheerleading for Obama and bashing of Clinton.

The Michelle Obama interview with Suzanne Malveaux that evening amounted to more positive press time for Senator Obama during the evening CNN broadcast with Mrs. Obama's avoidance of addressing the subject of Reverend Wright directly, instead stating that she and Obama were trying to move forward and leave the issue behind. Malveaux succeeded in shucking her responsibility as a serious agent of the news media on this occasion and did not press Mrs. Obama any further regarding the Wright controversy. Caroline Kennedy shared the interview stage with Michelle Obama and spoke about the involvement of women voters in the Democratic Party primaries. It was not really clear why Caroline Kennedy was present with Michelle Obama during the Malveaux interview, but viewers were left with the impression that Caroline Kennedy lent credibility to the sincerity of the Obamas wanting to distance themselves from Reverend Wright, remain positive, and move forward with the campaign.

The remainder of the evening broadcast on CNN, network correspondents overtly catered to the Obamas and repeatedly belittled and ridiculed Senator Clinton seemingly in an overt effort to aid Senator Obama with getting past the Reverend Wright controversy. In contrast, this was markedly a courtesy the news media failed to extend to Clinton during her struggle to move past the Bosnia sniper fire controversy.

TOXIC TACTICS:
Demonizing

To demonize is defined by the American Heritage College Dictionary as "to represent as evil or diabolic." This interpretation includes the act of being wicked, fiendish, or cruel. During the 2008 election season, the American news media used the toxic tactic of demonizing select individuals involved with the presidential election process as a means to ensure they were rendered less appealing to the voting populace. Any time a party nomination contender or party nominee, that was not favored by the news media, seemed to be gaining political ground or favor with voters, they immediately became the target of acute demonization from the news media which both criticized and scrutinized them in such a ruthless manner that a noticeable drop in opinion polls almost always indicated the tactic had a negative impact on both the candidate's image and campaign. The demonizing tactic was further used by the news media to increase drag on campaigns already experiencing difficulties or setbacks during the 2008 election season. When used in this form, the negative appeal of the candidate subject to this tactic of toxicity seemed to be multiplied in a manner that made a minor flaw in character such as a quick temper, or even a slip of the tongue seem like dropping the "f-bomb" from the pulpit during Sunday mass. Though this tactic was used in both covert and overt forms, both uses seemed to have an equally detrimental effect on the individual and campaign of whomever was subjected to its use.

The most frequent and overt use of demonizing during the '08 election season was undoubtedly against Senator Hillary Clinton when she could do or say almost nothing that the news media did not turn into something far more negative in nature. The same was true for former President Clinton who vigorously campaigned for her during her run for the Democratic Party nomination, but was hampered by the incessant scrutiny of the news media that unfairly characterized everything he did during the campaign as negative and even criticized him when he suggested the news media was going out of its way to demonize him and the Senator. Words used to describe or demonize Senator Clinton during regular coverage of the primary elections in both broadcast and written form included the terms negative, divisive, cut throat, and polarizing. The Senator was also, more than once, characterized as wanting "to become President so bad" that she would "stop at nothing" to obtain her lofty goal. Clinton's campaign ads were often referred to as "going negative"[19] when the content of them raised any question regarding the preparedness of Senator Obama to serve as President, though arguably negative statements issued by those associated with the Obama campaign directed at Clinton were described as completely in bounds and never characterized as being negative by the news media. Former President Clinton was frequently demonized by the news media in a manner that characterized him as having a "nasty temper" as well as possessing "baggage" that, though never completely explained, was said to have been an albatross to his wife's campaign for the party nomination for the presidency. Self appointed Obama surrogate and CNN regular/guest correspondent Roland Martin made reference to the issue of both Clintons possessing baggage in a commentary he wrote for the CNN Website titled: "Forget an Obama-Clinton or Clinton-Obama ticket."[20] The often controversial and brash Martin boldly stated in the commentary in regards to why the Obama-Clinton or vice versa dream ticket would not or *should* not come to fruition, "Obama would not want to carry Clinton baggage. He has offered a vision of change, and having to answer to the years of strife under the Clintons would be too much. An Obama run would be about going after Republicans and Independents, and Clinton being on the ticket would make that very difficult."[21] Adding insult to injurious statements made against the Clintons during the campaign season from correspondents like Martin, former President Clinton was further characterized by the news media as, according to "unnamed sources," engaging in unsavory activities while campaigning for Senator Clinton. This was never proven during the course of the campaign, but the mere mention of it during the election season was enough to cost Senator Clinton several points in opinion polls at the time and provided plenty of talking points for correspondents and journalists that seemed to hold deep contempt for the political power couple.

The more covert form of demonizing used by the news media during election season '08 was directed at Senator John McCain and his running mate, then Governor Sarah Palin, much later in the election season and on the heels of the party national conventions. When it seemed that McCain gained a slight bounce in the polls coming out of the Republican National Convention, the news media immediately began to produce articles and commentary that demonized him as hot headed even citing several cases where he used expletives when addressing political rivals directly. Several leading news media outlets posted a story written by Libby Quaid of the Associated Press referencing McCain's temper during the campaign season titled, "McCain's temper may prove to be a liability."[22] While McCain was not demonized as explicitly as the Clintons, the reference to his temper insinuated that he possessed acute emotional instability that could easily raise questions regarding his fitness to serve in the nation's highest office.

In October of 2008, *Newsweek* magazine published a cover and article describing Senator McCain as "Mr. Hot," making direct reference to his sometimes quick temper and characterizing him as "sometimes impulsive" and "unpredictable."[23] The corresponding cover of the magazine in which this article was published displayed a picture of McCain with a reddish hue facing in one direction as "Mr. Hot" while Senator Obama, on the same cover, faced the opposite direction with a bluish hue and was referred to more flatteringly as "Mr. Cool," as opposed to Mr. Cold which carried a much more negative connotation. McCain's Alaskan running mate, former

Governor Sarah Palin was also subject to demonization by the news media regarding the "Troopergate" scandal in her home state that, though it was never proven that she broke any laws through her involvement, the news media used to characterize her as a power freak that used her elected office to perform misdeeds against innocent citizens of Alaska. Later during the General Election campaign, the news media cited "inside campaign sources" that characterized Palin as "none cooperative," "going rogue," and "hard to deal with,"[24] while on the campaign trail for Senator McCain. She was also later described repeatedly by the news media as being, much like former President Clinton, "a drag on the ticket" for which she actively campaigned, as a vice presidential nominee.

Demonizing, as a toxic reporting tactic, was used recurrently by the American news media during the course of the 2008 campaign season to assassinate the characters of several individuals associated with our national election process. The act of demonizing in itself was bad enough, however when coupled with unequivocal bias in favor of an opponent, it had an even more lethal effect on candidates and their campaigns which, as a result, rendered the candidate's opponent a seemingly much better alternative. During future national elections, news media consumers should be wary of any coverage that takes on an overly negative tone in regards to only certain campaigns and individuals, especially if a given correspondent or journalist seems to express a personal contempt for either. News media consumers should further limit exposure to news media sources that are always negative toward the same individuals during a campaign as it is a dead giveaway that the Media Political Machine is working diligently to steer viewers and voters alike away from individuals and campaigns outside of its favor which just may happen to also be its chosen victor's most formidable opposition.

May 2008

Following the annual State of the Black Union Symposium attended by many members of the culturally and politically African American elite, *Vibe Magazine*, a popular hip hop culture and entertainment magazine published, "Don't Call It A Comeback,"[25] about Senator Hillary Clinton who happened to be one of the attendees of the symposium. Senator Obama declined the invitation to attend, however, he offered to send his wife to attend in his absence. The title of the story was a play on words in that it was the opening line of a popular rap song by L.L. Cool J in the early 1990s titled "Momma Said Knock You Out." The story addressed a serious controversy that was brewing within the African American community sparked by loyalty and support of Senator Clinton, wife of former President Clinton who was near and dear to the hearts of the vast majority of African Americans, versus support of Senator Barack Obama who was half black and one who many regarded as the first "serious black candidate" to run for the office of President of the United States. This controversy of who to support was so volatile that popular radio personality and activist Tavis Smiley, who was critical of Senator Obama for not attending the symposium, received threats from alleged Obamamaniacs.

On the heels of her address at the symposium, Clinton agreed to an interview with *Vibe* columnist Joan Morgan, an admitted Barack Obama supporter. In the interview, Clinton was asked a host of questions ranging from how she connects so easily to those she encounters, to what her candidacy represented for women. Morgan even pressed Clinton regarding receiving support from Black Entertainment Television (BET) founder, Bob Johnson, while the network (which he no longer owned) often, according to Morgan, portrayed women in a negative or degrading manner. Senator Clinton answered all questions with intelligence and grace as easily as when she engaged in heated debates with the well informed, prepared, and articulate Senator Obama during the primary elections. As Morgan quizzed Clinton on very serious issues surrounding Clinton's campaign for the Democratic nomination for the presidency, though an admitted Obama supporter, Morgan's words reflected the element of objectivity from the first words of her story to the very last. This was an element rarely, if ever seen during television news programs on leading networks as well as in articles written in news oriented magazines. If it was possible for a journalist for a hip hop entertainment magazine geared toward young African Americans, who was also a supporter of Senator Barack Obama during the 2008 elections, to remain objective in her delivery of a story largely about what Senator Hillary Clinton meant for African Americans and women during the election season, then why was it so hard for news journalists to reflect the same fairness and balance in their delivery during the same time period? The answer to the question was because the news media had motives other than the balanced and fair delivery of newsworthy facts for purposes of informing those concerned. It sought, instead, to abuse its power to exercise influence over the outcome of the primaries and General Election in 2008. Fortunately for voters, viewers, and readers alike, these actions were well documented throughout the elections and there were articles, transcripts, and footage proving the news media's unmistakable bias during the elections of 2008.

6 May 2008

On the CNN Situation Room evening broadcast, it was portentously declared by network correspondents that the Indiana primary election was a "must win" for Senator Hillary Clinton to justify her continued existence in the race for the Democratic Party nomination for president in 2008. Former White House correspondent, and Bush Administration sympathizer, John King led the negative spin charge by the news media on the network with his favorite prop, the electronic "magic" situation board which he cleverly used to visually communicate present and predicted standings of state primary elections as well as to track delegate and superdelegate counts. The board was "magic" in the sense that it could easily be manipulated to reflect anything toxic King and fellow correspondents chose it to.

On this night, CNN correspondents made the accusation that Senator Clinton was a magnet for "Conservative Democrats" which they backed with neither facts nor figures. This act committed by CNN correspondents amounted to nothing more than smearing

Clinton's political image on an evening that they knew countless numbers of decided as well as undecided voters would be watching by charging that Clinton's campaign "borrowed heavily from the Republican political playbook"[26] through using campaign tactics and terminology that is typically native to the Republican Party. Network correspondents specifically cited Clinton's comment that she would not hesitate to "obliterate" Iran if they used nuclear weapons against ally Israel. CNN Correspondent Carol Castellano stated regarding this charge against Clinton during the broadcast, "Despite that, and a family income of $100 million over the last seven years, Hillary Clinton is connecting with the blue-collar crowd, and some say she's done that by ripping a page from the Republican handbook."[27] Said another program guest, George Lakeoff of the University of California Berkeley about Clinton during the broadcast: "What she's doing in attacking Obama as an elitist is taking that Republican conservative strategy and using it against Obama as if she were a Republican candidate."[28] A CNN independent poll was then introduced which overwhelmingly indicated Clinton was employing negative campaign tactics against Senator Barack Obama. CNN reported it was their finding that the poll indicated the opposite results for Senator Obama. CNN, however, neglected to reveal particulars about the individuals polled or in what crafty manner questions were asked of those polled.

At around 6:30 pm, it was triumphantly announced that Barack Obama had a decisive win in North Carolina and the race had been called early in his favor. Curiously, however, in the case of the Indiana primary election, Senator Clinton was leading Senator Obama 57% to 43% with 20% of the vote being reported. Though it was obvious as past races had proven, the primary election in that state was virtually over, it was repeatedly said to be "still too early to call" as a victory for Senator Clinton. This allowed network correspondents a sizeable block of time to harp on Senator Obama's impressive win in North Carolina and what it meant for the "uphill battle" Senator Clinton faced in her quest to retake the delegate lead from Obama. Correspondent John King took toxic reporting lead during the broadcast with his personal preference electronic board, breaking the covered states down all the way to the level of precinct. He purposely held off announcing a Clinton in the state of Indiana while at the same time providing reasons for putting North Carolina in the win column for Senator Obama early on, because of Senator Obama's lead in the state at the time by a margin of 65% to 35%. This afforded the network the opportunity to go live to Raleigh, North Carolina to speak at length with Obama campaign strategists to continue spin in favor of Obama becoming the Democratic Party nominee to the General Election.

At 7:30 p.m. with 50% of the precincts reporting and Clinton maintaining a decisive lead over Obama in the Indiana primary race, CNN still refused to project a win for her, instead heaping more praise and attention on Obama and his win in North Carolina with John King offering the explanation that certain "key precincts" had still not yet reported as a reason for holding back on announcing victory for Clinton. A CNN payroll panel was then consulted regarding the evening's election results with John King and contributor Roland Martin, both of which who showed strong support for Obama over Clinton on past broadcasts. King again led the toxic barrage of bias mocking Clinton's argument that Florida and Michigan should be counted even after both states violated Democratic Party rules regarding the dates on which their elections were held. The usually conservative leaning King even went as far as to offer the empty rhetoric regarding what Obama should do to "seal the deal" and win the nomination which, citing King's past history of loyalty to the Bush Administration when reporting as a White House correspondent for the network, may as well have been Karl Rove offering Obama advice regarding steps he should take to win the nomination.

Also while viewers awaited the results from the Indian primary election to be announced, CNN aired a story focusing on several voting issues regarding a state law that required a government issued identification card to vote in state elections. This was an obvious covert attempt by the network to introduce controversy into the Indiana primary as if to say that a Clinton win could be the result of, in some manner, the disenfranchisement of citizens of Indiana by the voting process in the state. No such claims were reported in regards to the North Carolina election process. Immediately following this story, Senator Barack Obama's North Carolina victory speech was broadcast, taking place during prime air time while the majority of viewers were eagerly watching and listening for the evening's election results. Later in the evening, following the announcement that Senator Clinton had pulled off a narrow win in the Indiana primary election, a lone Clinton campaign strategist, Lanny Davis, was given air time during which he rebutted the rhetoric of John King and other Obama supporters rounding out the evening's panel. Davis did so handily, however, he was outnumbered by the Obama supporters that CNN stacked the deck with on the evening's broadcast. The mob of Obama supporters on the panel was also given the final word prior to each commercial break, leaving viewers with arguments supporting Obama fresh on their minds. Said one political blogger during the course of the primaries, who went by the name BrandingIron, on the "Now Public" Website which described itself as Crowd Powered Media: "the more I read online and the more I watched CNN and MSNBC—the larger cable news networks—the more I saw that Clinton victories were downplayed and Obama losses were shrugged off."[29]

7 May 2008

The following day, MSNBC News Website featured the following stories in the "Decision '08" section, focused on politics, on its home page: "Clinton says she is staying in", "NYT analysis: Clinton finds her options dwindling", Newsweek: "Clinton's case for continuing," NBC's Russert: "Obama has the nomination," Newsweek: "Obama's plan to end the race in Oregon," and "Mike Gravel in latest Obama Girl video." Directly below the column was a picture of Senator Barack Obama with his latest total delegate count displayed beside Senator John McCain's picture and nomination winning point total. McCain, of course, had long since clinched the title of presumptive nominee of the Republican National Party with a decisive victory over the closest party contender. Candidates Clinton, Edwards, Romney, and Huckabee were represented in name only with their delegate totals listed beside their names, giving the impression that since Senator Obama was pictured beside John McCain, already the Republican presumptive nominee, that he had all but been declared the Democratic Party's presumptive nominee though Obama, with a total delegate count of 1844, was still shy of the 2026 delegates needed to secure the nomination. No mention was made on the site regarding Clinton's recent primary victory in the state of Indiana which indicated she was, at the time, very much still in the race. On the same day, Yahoo News online featured a video in which Mitt Romney referred to Senator Clinton as a more formidable opponent than Senator Obama. No mention of this comment was made on CNN or MSNBC News broadcasts or Websites, even for the sake of argument, though the networks often raised the issue of electability in various forums. Discussions regarding the question of electability on both networks almost always favored Obama.

8 May 2008

On the heels of much abuzz regarding the assessment of many in the media that Senator Clinton should drop out of the race following her 6 May squeaker of a win in the Indiana Democratic primary race and loss to Senator Obama in the North Carolina primary race, Wolf Blitzer on CNN's Situation Room featured an exclusive interview of Senator Obama on the evening broadcast. The show seemed to be already looking past Senator Clinton, as if, as indicted by the MSNBC News Website a day earlier, Senator Obama had already clinched the party nomination. The questions asked by Blitzer of Obama cleverly suggested a General Election matchup between Senators Obama and McCain. CNN's Election Center evening broadcast continued to heap praise upon Senator Obama, as had become tradition, and highlighted comments made by him on the earlier broadcast interview with Blitzer, which almost immediately stirred up controversy with the McCain camp, ingeniously giving viewers the impression that Senator Clinton was no longer a factor in the Democratic Party presidential nomination race.

The level of balance in this broadcast was above normal for the network's coverage of the campaign, however, the focus of the broadcast was unequivocally another clever way the network employed to facilitate and focus on tensions between the Obama and McCain campaigns which, in turn, insinuated that Obama would indeed be the Democratic Party nominee for the presidency.

In addition to this, during the broadcast, cherry picked footage of Senator Obama was also played, showing the senator in a dark suit walking with a crowd of straphangers that surrounded him, looking staff-like, giving viewers a glimpse of what he may look like as President with members of his administration and closest advisors in tow as he walked to a random political engagement.

The covert point of the broadcast was driven home by several looks back during the evening at Obama's exclusive interview with Blitzer earlier in the day. The broadcast even included a sneak peek at the latest *Time Magazine* cover that featured yet another picture of Senator Obama with the title "And the winner is......." on the front cover,[30] which eminently signified the news media's coronation of him as the Democratic nominee for the General Election prior to the completion of the primary election process. Highly negative discussion also ensued on the broadcast regarding the idea that the "Clintons" somehow felt as if they had a "right" to the presidency and were not ready to give up their position as royalty in the Democratic Party in efforts to stir up hate and discontent for Hillary Clinton's effort to win the party nomination. Interestingly, the Media Political Machine failed to raise the issue of divine right in relation to the presidency of the United States when President George W. Bush was running for office some years before, following closely on the heels of his father's presidency.

9 May 2008

On MSNBC's news program "Morning Joe," Senator Clinton came under attack by the show's host and members of a panel regarding a statement she made while on the campaign trail regarding her assessment that distinctive demographic sections of the American populace had supported her during the primaries and others supported Senator Obama. It should have been clear to any person with even a modest educational background that Clinton was simply highlighting the existence of a coalition of voters that she felt were her base versus that of Senator Obama. The program host, however, with the help of hired panel hands, attempted to demonize Clinton for making the statement, citing what the media felt was her injecting the issue of race into the political campaign. Much like the day's broadcast on CNN, the network repeatedly showed footage of Senator Obama being interviewed by correspondent Brian Williams in which he was shown in a favorable light versus that of the story previously featured focusing on an embattled Clinton. Following this, Clinton campaign Chair Terry McAuliffe made a guest appearance on the show following a negative lead in by the host who quipped that McAuliffe would somehow spin the results of the most recent Democratic primary election results, and according to several appendages of the Media Political Machine, the grim outlook for the future of Senator Clinton's bid for the party nomination.

Later in the afternoon, MSNBC continued to lambaste Clinton, even going so far as to insinuate that she should give up her bid for the party nomination while highlighting a statement made by Congressman Rahm Emanuel of Illinois, a friend and advisor to Senator Obama, referring to him now as the "presumptive nominee" in a public statement. MSNBC used this as fodder to drive home their point, offering no counter perspective or positive aspects regarding Clinton's campaign bid, even with the input of a panel of four contributors. The broadcast was obviously heavily pro-Obama. No mention was made of a strategy Clinton could possibly use to persuade super-delegates to support her despite Obama being ahead in the delegate count leading up to the Democratic Party National Convention though panel members were all too eager to offer strategies the Obama campaign could use to "seal the deal." The network chose to completely ignore the fact that the same individual, Congressman Emanuel, whose words were used to lend credibility to the idea of Senator Obama's emergence as the Democratic Party presumptive nominee for the presidency, was from Obama's home state and that his favorable comments regarding him could have well be driven by self interest should Obama indeed win the presidency.

MSNBC's "Hardball with Chris Matthews" evening broadcast yielded no different or more balanced points of view with Matthews joining the media mob, even covertly questioning former President Bill Clinton's integrity following a clip of him defending Senator Clinton regarding her heavily scrutinized comments at one of his campaign stops. Matthews further mocked the former President while showing clips of him "wagging his finger" as Clinton made a point about what he perceived to be the news media's anti-Hillary campaign in efforts to sabotage her chances to win the Democratic Party nomination. Matthews then went on to make fun of Senator Clinton following the playing of a clip of CBS's Late Show with David Letterman with host, Letterman, making jokes at the senator's expense regarding her being heavily favored and leading the polls "in the state of denial," making a play on words relating to past and upcoming state primary elections. The same joke was told by late night comedians Conan O'Brien and Jay Leno.

Matthews switched gears only to add to the hype of a Senator Obama and McCain match up by focusing on barbs being traded at the time between the two campaigns, instigated the day before by the Media Political Machine.

TOXIC TACTICS:
Insinuation

The strong insinuation tactic was used so frequently by Media Political Machine television news networks during the 2008 election season that its thinly veiled connotations often times seemed to be as overt as just coming out and saying what was meant. Whenever the Media Political Machine desired to throw rocks at candidates or issues and hide its hands, insinuation was used to cast seeds of doubt and contempt in the minds of viewers and voters in the most liberal manner possible without crossing the line of media etiquette which was almost never observed. It seemed that this manner of toxic conveyance of information was most often used when the American news media desired to send a strong message to viewers without actually saying what it was they wanted to, but at the same time saying just enough to paint the ugly picture. Insinuation, as a toxic news reporting tactic, however afforded correspondents the element of plausible deniability whenever they felt the need to stir controversy that could possibly backfire on them or the network if careful attention was not given to what was acceptable to program viewers.

While there were many examples of the use of this highly lethal tactic during the '08 election season two cases in particular, one meant to bring into question an individual's character and integrity, and another meant to send a presidential hopeful a message, proved to be the most notable for the discriminating viewer. The first case of blatant insinuation meant to invoke memories of a scandal that once took place in American politics, occurred on 9 June 2008 at a time when it was critical that candidates maintained a positive image to remain in the race for the White House. CNN Correspondent Campbell Brown, who often unashamedly displayed her contempt for both Senator and former President Clinton during network broadcasts in election season 2008, made a comment directed at the former President in an attempt to bring into question his fidelity during the campaign season, or at least insinuate that it was a possibility that he was engaging in relationships with other women during Senator Clinton's campaign for the Democratic Party nomination. This use of toxic insinuation in news reporting was the grossest, most extreme, and tasteless of the entire campaign season. Brown's statement successfully negated the positive effects of any slogan referencing trust or balance in news reporting that the network that employed her could possibly have ever uttered. Her statement also introduced toxicity to the Hillary Clinton campaign for the presidency at a time in which negative press could cost Clinton big-time during future primary elections. Though Brown did not actually make the statement regarding the former President's alleged infidelity along the campaign trail, the effects of her insinuation were no doubt detrimental to the Hillary Clinton campaign which at the time was struggling to gain momentum against an Obama campaign that was picking up steam and additional support by the day.

The second case of extreme insinuation introducing toxicity in news reporting came in the days following Senator Obama's campaign trip to the Middle East to shore up his foreign relations experience prior to the Democratic National Convention and the General Election. When some appendages of the Media Political Machine felt left out after Senator Obama allowed three correspondents from CBS News to accompany him on his trip to provide exclusive coverage while access for numerous other news stations was limited at best. Following this action by the Obama campaign, a noticeable change in the type of coverage, from favorable to negative, that Senator Obama received was noted on several news networks. One of the most notable examples was a case of insinuation during news reporting which took place on CNN only days after Senator Obama's departure. It was well noted that the Senator, during his many campaign speeches during the election season, pronounced the words Taliban as and Pakistan in the same manner in which people of Middle Eastern descent do, which is, undoubtedly, the correct pronunciation of the terms versus the way in which the words are pronounced in Western society. Out of all the times Senator Obama uttered these words, attention was never drawn to his pronunciation of them, however, when it was noted that some news media entities were upset at being left out in the cold during Obama's Middle Eastern campaign trip, CNN aired a story closely focused on the way he pronounced the terms versus the way other American government leaders pronounced them. The story insinuated quite unmistakably that Senator Obama possibly identified more closely with Middle Eastern society than the average American, invoking memories of early allegations that Senator Obama was a Muslim by faith and attended Muslim schools as a child. This case of extreme insinuation was most evident due to the timing of and circumstances surrounding the airing of the story, giving strong indications that it was a part of an attempt by an arm of the Media Political Machine to send Senator Obama a covert message that it could change the tone of his coverage whenever it saw fit, negatively impacting his campaign as was often the case with Senator Clinton's campaign that eventually succumbed, in large part, due to overwhelmingly negative press coverage.

Though the use of strong insinuation as a toxic news reporting tactic was not used as frequently during the 2008 election season as most other tactics of introducing bias into serious news reporting, it was arguably one of the most detrimental to whomever it was used against. It should also be noted that this tactic was not as widely used among news media correspondents and was reserved, during the campaign season, for the boldest and most uncouth correspondents who injected strong partisan opinions into the stories about which they reported. The use of this tactic, especially during what was perhaps the most important election season of modern American history, reflected extreme disregard for everything democracy stands for as well as for the right of voters to make important choices based on the conveyance of factual information instead of biased news reporting in its most contemptuous and toxic state. The choice by agents of the news media to engage in personal attacks on individuals about whom they report, using underhanded tactics such as stringent insinuation, proved to be one of the most disdainful acts committed by the Media Political Machine, carrying untold ramifications for persons at the receiving end of such attacks.

The news media industry, as a whole, should do all that is in its power, whether through use of fines, administrative leave, or dismissal to prevent such toxic news reporting tactics from being used in *any* form during broadcasts as it does nothing more than discredit both the correspondent and news media network that employs it as agents of serious and "trusted" news reporting.

13 May 2008

Despite a landslide win by Senator Clinton in the West Virginia Primary, CNN continued its in your face reporting practices in support of Senator Obama. A photo of him setting up a behind the back, corner pocket shot on a pool table was displayed, and viewers were asked to submit a caption for the photo. The winner would receive an honorable mention on the broadcast and a t-shirt with some form of network advertising emblazoned on it. According to "CNN 360" host Anderson Cooper, the winning caption was: "nomination corner pocket," which was said to have been submitted by one of the show's viewers. Of course with the networks credibility issues for unbiased, serious news reporting, it could have just as easily been created in the network newsroom and tagged with a phony name to appear to have been submitted by some random viewer which was not at all beneath the toxic reporting tactics of the Media Political Machine. Following this, Correspondent John King was all too eager to break out his "magic board" once again in an attempt to persuade some easily influenced and ill informed viewers to believe that Senator Clinton's West Virginia primary win was meaningless because Senator Obama was too far ahead of Clinton in delegate and super-delegate totals for the state's primary results to matter.

CNN further made a stretch of an attempt to turn a key Mississippi congressional seat win by a Democrat, linked by Republicans to the Obama-Jeremiah Wright controversy, into a victory for Senator Obama due to the candidate successfully overcoming the alleged toxic association and claiming a political victory. Somehow, CNN correspondents equated the win by the Democrat to a victory for Obama clearly in efforts to minimize the effects of the 66% to 27% win by Senator Clinton over Senator Obama in the West Virginia primary election. On a night that should have clearly been dominated by talk of Senator Clinton being yet a formidable opponent for Senator Obama and very much still in the race for the nomination, CNN once again made it glaringly apparent that it was biased against her and in favor of an Obama nomination.

As the evening wore on, White House correspondent Suzanne Malveaux was brought on the show to weigh in on the issue of Obama being the projected nominee of the Democratic Party which she was all too inclined to do. Correspondent Jessica Yellin chimed in that the Clinton campaign was "disorganized" and did not run as efficiently as the Obama campaign even though she was a CNN embed with the Clinton campaign on the night of Clinton's West Virginia victory. One would have thought that Yellin might comment regarding the momentum of the campaign despite being behind in the nomination race or the drive and enthusiasm that Clinton campaign workers displayed in the heat of the tight race to the finish. Instead of attempting to show any semblance of balance in the broadcast by reflecting on each campaign favorably, CNN was demonstrably negative toward the Clinton campaign. This contrasted sharply against the backdrop of praises sung about the Obama campaign by its new friend in the news media, Suzanne Malveaux. During the broadcast, Yellin eagerly offered insight into alleged concerns among Clinton campaign staffers that were shared with her by, of course, campaign insiders that remained unnamed. "But they also talk about the fact that the campaign is a little disorganized and I am not going to make any friends over there by saying this, but the responsiveness of the Obama campaign, how efficient they are, how organized they are is in such stark contrast to the Clinton campaign, which is sort of... sometimes really runs well, and sometimes seems disorganized and this has *always* been the case,"[31] Yellin stated during the broadcast. Though this may have very well been the case in regards to the inner workings of the campaigns and as far as what some Clinton campaign workers felt, CNN made it obvious during the broadcast that it was going out of its way to bash the Clinton campaign while increasing favorable references to the Obama campaign. In case upon case of past political contests, news media correspondents have shown loyalty and favor to the campaigns with which they covered exclusively, *especially* those with which they were embedded. Yellin's highly negative comments regarding the Clinton campaign on this particular evening went a step further in proving the existence of a covert campaign on the part of the Media Political Machine to ensure the Clinton campaign received as much negative press time as was possible to aid the Obama campaign's efforts, though unwarranted, to achieve victory during the race for the Democratic Party nomination. During the remainder of the broadcast, several comments were made by various correspondents during the evening that the Clinton campaign possibly had regrets that it had not focused more on the caucus states earlier in the campaign. It was not, however, clear where they got this information from. It was also repeatedly impressed upon viewers that Senator Obama had "shifted gears" and had re-focused attention on John McCain as the presumptive Democratic nominee.

On the same evening, MSNBC followed suit by reporting on its broadcast of "After Hours" regarding the Democratic Congressional seat win in the state of Mississippi by Travis Childers, also attempting to detract from the effects of the Clinton win in West Virginia. The network successfully replaced Clinton's victory, through toxic news reporting and self interest, with a victory for Senator Obama instead of declaring the evening a victory for Childers or the Democratic Party. The evening's host and payroll panel members tried to lend credibility to political pundits and correspondents' deduction that it was "mathematically impossible" for Senator Clinton to win the party nomination at that point in the race. One panel member even went as far as to say that statements made by Clinton during her primary victory speech earlier in the evening was actually more of a concession speech because she made statements, read into by the news media, that she had not made in previous victory speeches. This amounted to nothing more than the Media Political Machine fishing for more reasons to suggest that Senator Clinton and her supporters had lost confidence themselves and in the Clinton campaign. From this, the conversation became how much Clinton's refusal to simply throw the towel in and quit the race for the nomination was "helping" the Obama campaign, because "people" were "beginning to resent her" for not giving up. Throughout the night, next to no focus was placed on the Clinton win in the West Virginia primary election because network correspondents instead focused on negative aspects of the Clinton campaign and her refusal to throw in the towel prematurely to make way for the party nomination of

Senator Obama.—So much for America's free democratic election process.

18 May 2008

One day following a toxic CNN news special focusing on Senator John McCain's age in regards to his bid for the Presidency, the network continued its love affair with Senator Obama with a report that focused on what was reportedly the largest crowd draw for a political event in U.S. history with some 50,000 people attending a campaign rally featuring the Senator in Oregon which reflected quite favorably on him. Senator Clinton's campaign for the party nomination was all but dropped from the news media topic agenda. Following the report, a brief mention was made regarding how well Senator Clinton was projected to do in the Kentucky Democratic primary race. Despite initial remarks that seemed favorable for Senator Clinton, the video clip that accompanied the story was one in which she aggressively spoke about sitting President George W. Bush kissing up to the Saudis and "begging" for increased oil production to help with lowering fuel prices in the U.S. The clip was just the sort that turned many voters away from supporting her, because it seemed that many did not approve of a woman speaking in such an aggressive manner. The playing of this clip, reversed the positive effects of initial favorable comments about Clinton at the start of the story.

This story was followed by reports of problems in the McCain campaign regarding his need to distance himself from President George W. Bush and Vice President Dick Cheney. There was also talk of a war chest merger between the Clinton and Obama campaigns complete with snide and degrading comments in reference to the Clinton campaign being "broke." Focus then turned to the crowd that came out to hear Senator Obama speak in Portland, Oregon that day. Media correspondents made several references to Obama having reached "rock star status," then the question was raised once again as to whether it was time for Senator Clinton to bow out of the presidential race as if to say that Senator Obama's ability to draw a large crowd of his own supporters was justification to question another candidate's right to remain a contender in the race for the party nomination in the world's leading democratic nation.

While CNN embarrassed itself and insisted upon doing more damage to its reputation as a serious and "trusted" news station by wasting valuable airtime through covering a ridiculous story regarding a parrot that was taught by its owner to say the name Barack Obama as well as one of his popular campaign slogans, MSNBC all but ignored Senator Clinton as a contender for the Democratic Party nomination even following her decisive victory over Senator Obama in the Kentucky Democratic primary election. The network did, however, underscore Clinton's defeat at the hands of Obama in the Oregon primary on the same night. Zoot suited MSNBC Correspondent Keith Olbermann featured a story regarding provocative statements made by Reverend John Hagee regarding Adolf Hitler's extermination of the Jewish people as biblical and led to the eventual establishment of an independent Jewish state. Olbermann further focused on Senator John McCain's relationship with the often controversial clergyman seemingly in an attempt to liken the relationship of the two public figures to that of Senator Obama's with Reverend Jeremiah Wright. The story insinuated that Senator McCain should formally and publicly cut ties with Hagee just as was required of Obama some weeks earlier. The facts of the matter, complete with an audio clip of Hagee making the statements in question regarding Hitler and the persecution of the Jews were a stretch of an attempt, at best, to bring the reputation of Senator McCain into question, making a weak case of guilt by association which stirred manufactured controversy nonetheless. This was, intriguingly, the same form of negative rhetoric used by MSNBC and CNN alike in discrediting the record of Senator Clinton, ridiculing her efforts to continue her campaign for the Presidency despite lagging behind Senator Obama in the delegate count for the Democratic Party nomination. The difference was now that the media had decided that Obama would indeed secure the nomination, the turrets had now turned on Senator McCain.

In sharp contrast, the evening's broadcast was interwoven with frequently played clips of Senator Obama giving a victory speech following his Oregon primary victory over Senator Clinton. After watching several other television news stations that same evening, no mention was made regarding the controversy surrounding Senator McCain and John Hagee which further proved the story to be nothing more than a cherry picked story that CNN aired to reflect negatively against Senator McCain as the Republican opponent Senator Obama would face if he in fact won the Democratic Party nomination.

25 May 2008

CNN: Special Investigations Unit featured a story hosted by Dr. Sanjay Gupta titled "The First Patient: Health and the Presidency."[32] The story featured an insider's view regarding the health status of several past Presidents of the U.S. while serving in the Oval Office. The story also focused some attention on the doctors who served them. It was immediately obvious that the airing of the program was a both bold and thinly veiled attempt at bringing the issue of Senator McCain's age and health into question to cast him in a negative light as possibly being too old, frail, or feeble to serve in the nation's highest elected office.

As expected, it was pointed out early on in the feature broadcast that Senator Obama was the youngest candidate for the presidency in 2008 at the age of 47, cunningly insinuating that due to his age in relation to the other candidates that he was viewers' best choice to support for the presidency. It was also pointed out, as the only low point in his record of health, that he was a former smoker who was able to kick the habit with pressure from his wife Michelle. Senator Clinton was also given a clean bill of health in the broadcast and it was mentioned that she had no known health issues of an adverse nature to report. As a caveat, however, it was ominously pointed out that "one never knows" what type of health issues could crop up in the future for a presidential candidate, which was a negative slant regarding the issue that was not mentioned when Dr. Gupta spoke regarding the health of Obama. The story continued by focusing on the health of past Presidents FDR, Ronald Reagan, Woodrow Wilson, Grover Cleveland, and of course JFK, all of who experienced significant medical issues during their terms as President of the U.S. This part of the story strategically insinuated, as with its focus on the frailty of Presidents Wilson and Roosevelt during their presidencies that there was a direct correlation between their age and the health complications they faced which was often "covered up" by White House staffers as was the case with Ronald Reagan's battle with the early effects of Alzheimer's Disease during his second term. Gupta's keying in on Ronald Reagan's age and mental health condition, as the nation's oldest President to serve in the Oval Office, instantly stirred a concern in regards to Senator McCain's fitness to serve as the nation's President at his age. It should also be noted that only one day prior, it was pointed out during a prime time broadcast on the network that though Senator McCain's mother was still quite spry at the ripe age of ninety-six years of age, his father died at age seventy, insinuating the senior Senator was likely on borrowed time. Though the broadcast was very informative and interesting, the purpose and timing of the show was keeping with CNN's track record for favoring Senator Obama's candidacy for the President of the U.S., which grossly took away from any academic purpose for airing the story. Host Sanjay Gupta concluded the story by stating that viewers were presented with the facts during the broadcast and it was now up to them to decide who was the "most fit" candidate for the presidency, which was essentially a no-brainer insinuation when comparing a physically fit 47 year old to a much older candidate with multiple documented cases of melanoma on file as was distinctively pointed out in many CNN broadcasts during the latter half of the election season.

27 May 2008

CNN's "Anderson Cooper 360" focused part of its segment on statements made recently by former President Bill Clinton at a campaign rally in support of Senator Clinton. Statements made by the former President outlined his assessment that there was a conspiracy afoot, being orchestrated by an unnamed party, that sought to sabotage the Hillary Clinton campaign for the presidency through leading voters to believe that Senator Obama was a better choice for the Democratic Party nomination, and through overtly smearing her as well as dismissing her as a serious candidate. After a clip of the former President making these comments while standing in the bed of a big red pickup truck with a large American flag in the background was played, Cooper ushered in a panel of three, comprised of former White House Correspondent Candy Crowley, CNN Senior Political Analyst Gloria Borger, and another random CNN contributor. After asking several questions of the panel members regarding the former President's accusations, it became evident that there was no balance on the panel regarding this issue even on the part of Cooper. Each member of the panel did however agree that this was an attempt on the part of the Clinton campaign to distract viewers and voters from Clinton's lagging behind Senator Obama in the delegate count for the party nomination. The exhibition of the completely biased panel and correspondent was one of CNN's boldest and most overt uses of rhetoric to discredit the words of the former President and Senator Clinton, dismissing the two as whining about an issue that was not really there, possibly because they pointed an accusing finger squarely at the news media. Ironically, however, by virtue of there being absolutely no balance or opposing viewpoint despite the presence of three panel members to provide commentary regarding the story, it was readily apparent that what the former President was saying was not all in his head and the Media Political Machine had pulled out all the stops to maintain its cover as a covert operative in the elections of 2008.

TOXIC TACTICS:
The Payroll Panel

The lopsided panel, also known as the "Payroll Panel" reigned supreme during election season 2008 as the most frequently used method of toxic news reporting on at least two of the most popular news networks on American cable television. The networks that most frequently employed this tactic used and re-used hand selected news media staff, or panel puppets, posing as subject matter experts on both American politics and the race for the presidency. The problem with this was the fact that the exact same panel members, obviously on the network's payroll, were consulted night after night regarding the latest happenings in the Democratic and Republican Party primary elections as well as in the days leading up to the General Election. You name the issue, they were experts on it. This included the economy, homeland security, rising gas prices and health care woes. Instead of bringing in a variety of panel members who were truly experts in their fields such as economists and educators, bankers and health care administrators, news media networks chose to consult the same old panel members, who just happened to most often be other media correspondents, to provide insight and commentary on the topic of the day. It only took the viewing of three or more broadcasts, however, to realize the panel was unmistakably "on the take" and a part of the Media Political Machine's effort to persuade viewers to think one way or the other regarding a given issue, or support one candidate over another during the primaries and in the General Election. The most prominent problem with the "Payroll Panel," aside from the obvious, was the illusion of balance the networks attempted to display in the makeup of the panel, being some in favor of an issue and some against. Upon closer inspection of the positions each panel member took regarding certain issues or candidates during the 2008 elections, however, it became apparent that in most cases the deck was stacked four to one in favor of or against a given issue or candidate, determined by the network's position. The lone voice on the panel that represented the opposing viewpoint, by design, was easily drowned out and overshadowed by virtue of being grossly outnumbered even as all were given roughly equal amounts of time in which to speak or present arguments in support of their *chosen* position.

The other glaringly apparent flaw having to do with the "Payroll Panel" was the practice by the news media networks featuring this information manipulation tool, of comprising discussion panels of its own news correspondents or those from associate news media outlets. The problem with this lies with the fact that since the correspondents were literally on the full time Media Political Machine payroll, they most often agreed with one another and towed the news media party line on any given issue. This form of panel assembled to discuss various issues, most often, did not provide further intellectually inclined insight into the issues, but instead reflected the concerted effort of news media representatives attempting to persuade others to think as they did, thus covertly robbing viewers of their ability to make informed decisions based on balanced news reporting. This practice left viewers with a distorted and unclear view of what was factual information versus what was largely spin-driven opinion.

Viewers should vigilantly guard themselves against this toxic method of news reporting, because while the existence of a panel in news reporting symbolizes the presence of subject matter expert involvement and opposing views, this is not the case of late. One only has to listen closely to the words of individuals making up a "Payroll Panel" to hear the chimes of rhetoric, self interest, and ill intent. Careful dissection of the words of these toxic panel members and attention to detail regarding their like positions on issues reveals they are all in tune with one another, and keeping time with the ever changing rhythm of the Media Political Machine.

2 June 2008

On the eve of the final Democratic Primary election, CNN came full force in all but holding a New Orleans styled funeral march for the Hillary Clinton campaign for the presidency in 2008. The evening broadcast of Anderson Cooper 360 was filled with commentary by Candy Crowley, David Gergen, and Gloria Borger regarding the dismissal of Senator Clinton as a contender in the presidential race, and what was next for her following Senator Obama becoming the presumptive nominee of the Democratic Party. Statements were made and choice sound bites were played, all lending credibility to their case for her to concede in the upcoming days in order for Senator Obama to go into the Democratic National Convention uncontested.

Former President Bill Clinton was dragged into the fray following inflammatory statements he made in response to highly offensive and disrespectful statements made by *Vanity Fair's* Todd Purdum in his hit piece titled "The Comeback Id,"[33] that would doubtfully have been tolerated by any stretch of the imagination if said about sitting President George W. Bush, or any past President. Former President Jimmy Carter was arguably treated with the same manner of disrespect most recently, following his choice to hold talks with Islamic extremist group, Hamas, in an attempt to broker a peace agreement between the organization and the Israeli government. There once was a time when former Presidents of the United States were treated with the respect commanded by a holder of the highest office in our nation's government. This seems to have changed markedly during and after the presidency of Bill Clinton and evidenced by an article written about him in *Vanity Fair* by Todd Purdum in which he used "unnamed sources" to accuse Clinton of being a womanizer on the campaign trail among other things which amounted to nothing more than another personal attack on the former President, with hopes of painting him as a political liability to Hillary Clinton's campaign bid for the presidency. Purdum completely dismissed a Presidential legacy that made that of President George W. Bush seem like a very bad dream that the nation could not wake up from. "........four former Clinton aides told me that, about 18 months ago, one of the president's former assistants, who still advises him on political matters, had heard so many complaints about such reports from Clinton supporters around the country that he felt compelled to try to conduct what one of these aides called an 'intervention,' because the aide believed, 'Clinton was apparently seeing a lot of women on the road,"[34] Purdum wrote. This statement alone had all the markings of one that was fabricated in the newsroom, and was highly indicative of the underhanded tactics the Media Political Machine skillfully used during the 2008 national elections to neutralize the former President's effectiveness on the campaign trail. Despite being a story that was obviously politically motivated and 99.9% smear tactic, CNN reported the story as credible. Even if it was (there was nothing tangible in the lines of the story to prove that it was), one would have to wonder about the timing of its release.

When former President Clinton responded to the words of the smearing article at the latest campaign rally for Senator Clinton, CNN once again took his words and ran with them as what they touted as "another rant" from the former President who was once again "showing his nasty temper," even though the audio tape of the former President's actual words were unavailable for viewers to hear for themselves. Clinton's response to the inexcusably disrespectful article was described as "nasty" while at the same time, news media crony Purdum was praised on the broadcast as both a serious and reputable reporter by CNN correspondent Gloria Borger.[35]

CNN then intensified the rhetoric through drawing the stretch of a conclusion that due to the latest allegations of infidelity on the campaign trail made against the former President by "unnamed sources," as well as Clinton's "nasty" response to the allegation, that he was too much of a political liability for Senator Clinton to even be considered as a running mate for Senator Obama if he became the Democratic Party's presidential nominee. CNN Senior Political Analyst, David Gergen, weighed in with yet more negativity in reference to the former President's "nasty temper" as if Clinton had not been smeared enough during the broadcast. "Because the question of the dream ticket partly revolves around: how about Bill? How does he fit into the picture? If you are Barack Obama sitting in the oval office, is Bill Clinton going to go off like Vesuvius at some point?" Gergen stated. This yet again brought into question the network's credibility as a "trusted" and "respected" news media entity due to inimitably lopsided reporting, ridiculing the Clinton campaign and completely ignoring Senator McCain while heaping more and more praise on Senator Obama and applauding him for his narrow lead over Clinton going into the final Democratic primary elections.

4 June 2008

Following Senator Clinton's news media facilitated loss to Senator Barack Obama in her bid for the Democratic Party nomination, *Time* magazine (in partnership with CNN), Senior Writer, Joe Klein, wrote an article calling for Clinton to immediately throw her support behind Obama to unite the party. Klein's article, titled, "Can Hillary Unite the Party?"[36] was a quite unflattering piece that largely focused on Clinton's faults and her campaign's shortcomings as was one of the Media Political Machine's documented party platforms throughout the primary election period. The article was merely the news media's latest edition to an already voluminous effort to trash both Clintons during Hillary's campaign yet twist their arms for use of their arsenal of political tactics and connections to support the Obama campaign, now that of the Democratic Party's official presumptive nominee. Klein opened the story by telling of a downtrodden Caucasian woman named Margaret who spoke to Clinton briefly along the campaign trail regarding her support and need for Clinton's proposed universal health care plan. After overhearing the woman tell her story to Clinton, Klein wrote that he approached the woman to hear the story again, personally, which she told him in a somewhat less dramatic fashion. Klein wrote that the woman also added a crude joke at the end of the version of the story she told him regarding how she was faring with her current health care insurance plan. Klein then distastefully and mockingly speculated in the lines of his story about what Senator Clinton's reaction would have been to the joke had she heard it.

In regards to the biased manner in which the story was written, when speaking regarding the Obama campaign, Klein made it a point to use favorable terms such as "young" and "brilliant" to describe Obama campaign staffers. Klein also, ironically, introduced the element of race into the article which was something deemed as taboo by the news media when Hillary Clinton made a comment during her campaign regarding the breakdown in demographics of her supporters versus those of Senator Obama. Clinton's comment was then referred to by the Media Political Machine as both "race baiting" and "playing the race card." Despite the media crying foul regarding this statement during the Democratic primary elections, Klein boldly wrote in his article about the success of the Obama campaign: "His army of young idealists, the brilliant organizers who had built his campaign from the ground up in Iowa and elsewhere, had won this nomination fair and square, and his nervously proud African-American supporters—never far from tears—were every bit as moving as Clinton's suffering Caucasians."[37] What was interesting was the fact that it was perfectly alright for the news media to bring up race in reference to the elections, however, any time Senator Clinton or the former President made even a fleeting reference to the element of race during the elections, the news media screamed bloody mass murder as if our nation's citizens were all the same size, shape, color and held the exact same political views. By now, the news media was frequently displaying a very clear pattern for toxic bias and rampant hypocrisy regarding the presidential candidates, the issues important to the American people, and the way it covered them to advance its own agenda of ill intent.

The remainder of the Klein's article, aimed squarely at hanging the fate of the Democrats and the outcome of the General Election on the shoulders of Senator Clinton, strangely characterized her as being responsible for uniting the party that the Media Political Machine blamed her alone for creating a rift within simply because she refused to abandon the will of the eighteen million Americans that supported her. "The sad reality is, though, that the coalition will have a chance to coalesce only if Hillary Clinton blesses the union,"[38] Klein wrote, completely dismissing the capability of American voters to make their own educated decisions regarding for whom to vote based on the issues and ideals most important to them. This pointed statement also curiously marked the beginning of the news media's efforts to strong arm the Clintons into campaigning as vigorously for the Obama campaign as they did for Senator Clinton's though they were often criticized for doing so and hamstringed from campaigning in her favor to their fullest potential by correspondents and journalists who were highly critical of their every move. In addition to this, Klein made a point to pick apart the speech Senator Clinton made on the night of Senator Obama's landmark primary victory, which gave him the required number of delegates necessary to become the Democratic Party's presumptive nominee. Klein minced no words in characterizing Clinton's speech that evening as "ungracious," "solipsistic," and "disappointing."[39] What Klein failed to recognize was perhaps Clinton felt it necessary, during her speech, to continue to display an image of strength to the millions upon millions of those who faithfully supported her through hell, high water, and relentlessly biased press coverage instead of immediately kneeling to kiss the ring of a victorious Senator Obama as the news media would have had it. In addition, as a serious contender for the Democratic Party nomination for the presidency, Senator Clinton probably had not planned to give a decisive concession speech on this particular night, because she had all intentions of pulling off an eleventh hour upset. This fact, however, was of no concern to the news media that felt she was not exiting, stage left, quickly enough. Klein's inclination to moreover characterize Clinton's pre-concession speech as a "graceless denouement"[40] also reflected the tendency of agents of the news media to abandon any facade of objectivity and professionalism to instead make repugnant personal attacks on any candidate who opposed their chosen candidate for the presidency in 2008.

As a follow up to the Media Political Machine's ever hastening timeline for her exodus from presidential race, Senator Clinton was raked over the coals by almost every major news media entity in the days that followed for not immediately giving her official concession speech. With the publishing of this article, Joe Klein reflected the unbridled bias and toxicity that was the trademark of the American news media, during the 2008 elections, as shamelessly as *Time* magazine, devoted a record number of magazine covers to the image of Senator Obama for the purposes of towing the Media Political Machine's party line of openly supporting him for the presidency while simultaneously cashing in on his popular image and boosting its ratings and sales.

Despite the contempt displayed so prominently and commonly by the American news media against Senator Hillary Clinton and her campaign for the Democratic Party nomination for the presidency, and following such brazenly biased news stories written by journalists eager to see a Clinton kneel before the now uncontested presumptive nominee for which they openly campaigned, Clinton's former hometown newspaper painted a more balanced picture of her departure from the hard fought race. The *Arkansas Democrat Gazette's* Alex Daniels published a story on the cover of the newspaper's Sunday edition titled, "Clinton calls it quits, puts her bid on ice,"[41] that reflected the realism of her defeat, yet left the punditry to the media big top's main performers. Though Daniels highlighted many quotes made by Clinton during her official bittersweet concession speech a day before, it was obvious that his story lacked the normal tone of news media hatred for the Clintons which was displayed in an unprecedented manner during the Democratic primary elections. This may have been due to his being a former supporter of hers while she was yet a contender for the nomination or perhaps simply the reflection of the professionalism of a truly serious journalist who refused to compromise his own integrity or that of his field by injecting personal bias or toxic spin into his story in efforts to demonize Clinton for acting as a stumbling block to the efforts of the Media Political Machine to crown its chosen victor and get on with the General Election race. In any case, the story exhibited the sharpest of contrasts through its use of unabridged factual information to explain the occurrence of Clinton's concession effort free of innuendo, insinuation, or bold faced contempt that made the employers of such news reporting tactics seem as amateurs and in a race for who could be the most biased and uncouth in delivery. "Today, as I suspend my campaign, I congratulate him on the victory he has won and the extraordinary race he has run. I endorse him and throw my full support behind him,"[42] Daniels quoted Clinton as saying. Unfortunately these words were not enough to satisfy the American news media, angered by the delay of the concession speech, and the Media Political Machine immediately began to over-analyze whether her words were "sincere" and whether or not she was "truly committed" to supporting Obama following her news media facilitated elimination from the presidential race.

9 June 2008

On the evening broadcast of "Your Money Your Vote," host Campbell Brown and obvious network selected, Obama supporting panel members, overwhelmed viewers with more favorable press time for Senator Obama and more negative press for Senator Hillary Clinton and former President Bill Clinton. Brown impertinently referred to the former President during her broadcast repeatedly as simply "Bill" in a blatant effort to minimize his role as former President and one of the most influential Democratic politicians of modern American history. The broadcast was curiously marked by an obvious attempt to in no way acknowledge Clinton's role as former President as if he never served as the nation's chief executive. Brown even went so far as to openly mock the former President by making the snide remark that he was "back to his old ways," quickly interjecting, "but it's not what you're thinking,"[43] as a lead in to a story she featured regarding Clinton following a commercial break. Brown's comment instantly evoked memories of the Monica Lewinsky scandal that dogged the former President during his second term in office, and more recent tales of infidelity of an alleged nature.

The crux of the night's broadcast focused on Brown and the evening's payroll panel re-heating the leftovers of Senator Clinton's concession speech following Senator Obama reaching the finish line in regards to the number of delegates needed to secure the party nomination some days before. They further delved into exactly what her role would be now in relation to the Obama campaign for the presidency. Brown played a clip of Senator John McCain making the point that the media "was not kind" to Senator Clinton during the campaign, and offering praises to her for what she did for the Women's Movement during her campaign for the presidency. Following the playing of the clip, one of Brown's panel members straight away dismissed McCain's comments, quite unsympathetically, as pointless, and stated in short that Senator Clinton's supporters should come to the realization that "she *lost*" and Senator Obama was the Democratic Party candidate for the General Election.

The final major story of the evening's broadcast focused on even more scrutiny of former President Clinton's response to yet another attack on his character by the news media from a writer for *Vanity Fair* magazine, a story that broke a week earlier. It was evident that the purpose of the re-hash of the story by Campbell Brown and CNN was to continue the assault on the Clinton name and legacy by focusing on the former President's often agitated responses to this form of personal attack rather than what caused him to react in the manner that he did. During the broadcast, Brown repeatedly referred to Clinton's response regarding this particular personal attack leveled by the *Vanity Fair* writer, again highly disrespectfully, as a "temper tantrum."[44] Brown then initiated an analysis of what the former President's role would be leading up to the Democratic Party National Convention and General Election now that Senator Clinton had been presumptively defeated by Senator Obama in the party nomination process. Though the former President had already returned to the helm of his foundation following the final primary contest between Senator's Obama and Clinton, even speaking to the United Nations regarding several issues of significance on the world stage, CNN succeeded in focusing more attention on the former President's reason for campaigning so vigorously for his wife, suggesting he was driven by self interest and wanted to make history by serving as both President of the nation and the spouse of the U.S. President as if somehow the latter would become the crowning achievement of his political career. The claim, of course, was not supported by facts. This latest attack on the Clintons by the network, under the pretense of "no bias, no bull" reporting, reaffirmed the existence of a both clandestine and widespread news media campaign with a mission not only to facilitate the elevation of Senator Obama's image in the eyes and minds of program viewers, but also to ensure that Senator Clinton had no chance of *ever* serving as President of the United States.

Finally, toward the end of the program, viewers were asked to come up with clever captions for a photo of Senator Obama riding a bicycle with an attachment with which he pulled his daughters along for a ride. The winning caption, said to have been sent in by a viewer, and selected as the winner by the network was: "finally the training wheels are off and the real race can begin." Correspondent Campbell Brown then went on to emphasize, in an overly favorable manner, some of the points made by Senator Obama earlier in the day to an audience of supporters regarding the economy.

TOXIC TACTICS:
The Negative Lead In

Another toxic reporting tactic employed by the American news media during the 2008 primary elections and in the days leading up to the General Election was the "Negative Lead In." This tactic was a very basic means of placing a negative spin on a cable news story prior to its being aired. It paid major dividends to the networks that most liberally employed it, and inflicted much damage to the image of numerous candidates and campaigns during the '08 election season. Though the tactic was used frequently by countless agents of the news media during the election season to plant seeds of deceit and trepidation in the minds of program viewers and voters alike, it was used most often and skillfully by news correspondents at CNN that implemented the tactic whenever it was necessary to ensure viewers were left with a negative impression of whomever or whatever a given story was about. The way the tactic worked was simple. Just prior to a news correspondent taking the broadcast to a commercial break, he or she gave viewers a teaser or preview of what feature story would follow the break. During that preview, the correspondent injected bias, toxicity, and or negative innuendo into the delivery to give viewers a negative impression of the individual or issue on which the upcoming story focused. Viewers were then allowed to mull over the contents of the negative preview or lead in during the commercial break, and naturally viewed the story through a jaundiced eye when it finally aired following the commercial break. The correspondent reporting on the story could then either inject more negativity into the story through his delivery of it following the commercial break, compounding its negative appeal, or use a more objective approach to conveying the story, because the negative teaser or lead in prior to the commercial had already cast a cloud of negativity over the story prior to its being reported.

Though numerous cases of the employment of the "Negative Lead In" by the news media were noted during the 2008 election season, perhaps the most notable and extreme use of the tactic took place only days following Senator Barack Obama officially becoming the presumptive nominee of the Democratic Party. On 9 June, 2008, CNN Correspondent Campbell Brown, who often openly displayed a bitter contempt for several individuals associated with political campaigns during the election season, used the negative lead in tactic regarding a story to air after a commercial break as she hosted an evening broadcast of "Your Money Your Vote." Brown snidely commented, as a toxic lead in to a story about former President Clinton, that he was "back to his old ways," then quickly interjected, "but it's probably not what you're thinking." Because the remark was made at a time when image was still critical to the Hillary Clinton campaign, Brown no doubt knew full well the impact that her statement could have as it stirred memories of the Monica Lewinsky scandal and followed closely on the heels of a recent accusation of infidelity on the part of the former President while on the campaign trail for his wife. While the corresponding story was far short of being negative or scandalous, the mere insinuation of infidelity on the part of the former President put a negative spin on the story as well as hung yet another media manufactured cloud of negativity over the Hillary Clinton campaign at a time when she least needed it and could have been still considered for the number two spot on a ticket now headed by Senator Obama.

The "Negative Lead In" was a toxic reporting tactic employed by the broadcast news media to shroud stories in a cloak of negativity even before they were aired, and deal damaging blows to the characters of individuals and political campaigns throughout the elections of 2008. In future election seasons, program viewers and voters should recognize the employment of the "Negative Lead In" tactic and beware of the toxic message it sends. The news media's decision to both employ and tolerate such toxic reporting tactics during the 2008 elections acutely reflected its devotion to self interest and the abandoning of its duty and responsibility to give the conveyance of newsworthy facts priority over uttering damaging insinuations and innuendo as lead ins to stories with which the voting populace were concerned.

10 June 2008

Deciding to take a break from the big top networks of news reporting, instead of being bombarded with the personal opinions of correspondents who want to mold the political ideology of viewers whom in many cases possess education levels beyond high school or a mere bachelor's degree in journalism, I spent part of the morning watching C-SPAN's "Washington Journal." Within the first few minutes of the broadcast, I picked up on vast differences in the style of reporting that left me feeling as if the mind control device of the Media Political Machine had been unlocked and lifted from atop my head. One of the most prominent differences in the manner of news reporting noted was that the host, a distinguished looking and serious African American gentleman who was simply referred to as "Rob," did not insult the intelligence of program viewers by forcing his personal views on them relating to stories he covered. Rob also refrained from presenting in a manner that placed more of the focus on him and the designer clothing he had on that day than the stories he delivered. It was further notable that his manner of reporting was not the "hey look at me" style of reporting I had become accustomed to seeing on almost all other news media television networks that often led me to believe some correspondents were more interested in campaigning for the Pulitzer Prize than in being serious news reporters. One other significant difference in the manner of news reporting Rob displayed was the fact that he actually interviewed someone other than another network correspondent, a regular contributor to his program, or a panel of various news media talking heads posing as subject matter experts on issues surrounding the failing economy and the upcoming General Election.

The featured guest on the show at the time of my viewing was Republican Congressman John Micah of Florida's 3ʳᵈ Congressional District who educated viewers regarding a 14.4 billion dollar appropriations bill being proposed in the U.S. House of Representatives, for Amtrak, that would afford the historic rail transportation company the ability to modernize rails, trains, facilities, and equipment in efforts to expand use of rails for commuting in order to alleviate stresses on household income due to soaring fuel prices. After laying out a host of facts and details about the bill and its purpose, which I found to be intellectually stimulating, the Congressman then entertained calls, some of which were quite hostile, from everyday working Americans, answering questions they had regarding this bill and other related political issues ranging from energy efficiency to current economic woes. Following this, Rob read some choice articles from various newspapers, and fielded more calls from viewers on Democrat, Republican, and Independent call lines seeking to voice their sentiments regarding the articles from which he quoted. Not once did Rob interject his own opinion regarding any of the issues he covered. He instead relegated his role to conveying the news as it was presented to him, allowing viewers the freedom to think for themselves and voice a position regarding subjects discussed.

Soon after fielding several calls from viewers regarding the quoted articles, Rob was joined on the show by Independent Congressman Bernie Sanders of Vermont who spoke to program viewers regarding the current energy cost crisis in the U.S., offering expert intellectual insight regarding issues important to Americans versus the heavily biased, entertainment oriented form of commentary often delivered by pundits on the payroll at other leading news networks.

TOXIC TACTICS:
The Mirror Interview

During some of the most critical and controversial periods of the 2008 election season, the news media airwaves were saturated with the toxic, lopsided coverage of stories that viewers and voters were most interested in. Apart from the complete lack of objectivity exhibited by leading news media correspondents while covering stories during the elections, the toxicity of each broadcast was also marked by the absence of opposing viewpoints due to the practice of guest appearances made by the same personalities over and over again. What was more was the fact that the personalities that most leading news media networks chose to employ as panel puppets, charged with the task of co-signing for everything the host correspondent uttered, just happened to also be, in most cases, network correspondents themselves. Network correspondents that hosted shows airing earlier or later in a network's broadcast line up, made frequent appearances on multiple broadcasts throughout the day during the 2008 election season. This action gave the appearance of objectivity and the façade of a correspondent soliciting the input of subject matter experts regarding some of the most important issues during the 2008 elections. It could easily be asserted that a correspondent standing in front of a mirror and interviewing himself would have had the same effect as correspondents, employed by the same news media entity, interviewing each other since there was seldom ever a case when they disagreed, presented opposing points of view, or strayed from the obvious news media party line.

The "Mirror Interview" was a toxic news reporting tactic used throughout the 2008 campaign season on leading news networks. It aided agents of the Media Political Machine with swamping program viewers with redundancy of perspective regarding various issues using the veneer of balance and objectivity through consultation with others. Unfortunately for viewers and voters alike, instead of soliciting the opinions or views of true subject matter experts, the news media craftily used the opinions and views of network cronies to drive home their toxic points in efforts to sway opinions prior to multiple elections in 2008. This toxic manner of news reporting cannot be trusted, as it is almost always completely devoid of objectivity due to the lack of opposing points of view when employed. A useful safeguard to protect oneself from falling victim to the "Mirror Interview" toxic news media tactic is to seek outlets for newsworthy information that do not rely heavily or solely on the opinions of people employed by that broadcast entity, but instead invites outside sources and actual subject matter experts to weigh in on important issues in the news as in the case of news media entities like C-SPAN.

11 June 2008

I was immediately re-introduced to the blatant bias of MSNBC news reporting by correspondent Keith Olbermann who chose CBS correspondent Katie Couric as his choice for the pointless nightly "worst person in the world," rant on the evening's broadcast of "Countdown with Keith Olbermann."[45] Couric, who has often been regarded as one of the best news correspondents on cable television and as always performing her duties with acute professionalism and class, was selected for this both unflattering and undeserved smear award for nothing more than daring to point out that Senator Hillary Clinton received an unprecedented amount of negative press coverage during her campaign for the Democratic Party nomination for the presidency. Couric asserted that Clinton was demonstratively more heavily scrutinized than any other candidate during the primary elections which was re-affirmed by the anger of many of her most loyal supporters who felt cheated by the efforts of the Media Political Machine to sabotage and destroy her campaign. Olbermann went on to ridicule Couric for talk of her possibly losing her job as host of the CBS Evening News due to low ratings. Comments Olbermann made during the broadcast regarding this had absolutely nothing to do with Couric's comments stressing the news media's ill treatment of Clinton. This form of criticism was coming from a person who spent much of his career as a sports news reporter and was now posing as one of MSNBC's leading correspondents and subject matter experts on American politics.

13 June 2008

During the course of writing this work, as irony would have it, the nation was both shocked and saddened to hear that a prominent member of the dwindling number of the serious and balanced news media old guard, NBC's "Meet the Press" host, Tim Russert died suddenly of a heart attack at age 58. It seemed as if the ranks of the unbiased news media correspondents was growing fewer in number by the day, and the hope that I had for a return to the old way of news reporting free of irrelevant antics, ratings grabbing entertainment, and self interest driven spin was fading fast. As I watched Wolf Blitzer and other correspondents interview each other and deliver words of support for Russert's family, then vividly describe how they all came to know him, I wondered if any of them understood how much he meant to the dignity and respect for pure, unadulterated news reporting. I wondered if any of them learned from him that it is possible to convey the news with intelligence, flair, and style while at the same time remaining neutral and impartial when confronting the most political, polarizing, or controversial issues, allowing for viewers to exercise freedom of thought to formulate their own opinions in regards to those issues. I wondered if any of them realized what a significant loss this was for the citizens of America and the news media alike. I hoped that somehow one of them would take a minute as a result of his sudden death to see that they were all becoming a part of the machine and were in danger of compromising viewers' respect for and confidence in the form of news reporting that was the trademark of those like Russert who paved the way for a great number of them.

Not only was this a dark day for the news correspondents and networks, Russert's death marked a dark day for freedom and democracy due to the inevitability of the ushering in of a new form of journalism and news reporting that is on track to become the standard across the board. His death also sadly marked the end of an era of the craft of news reporting in its purest, fair, balanced, and most trusted form.

16 June 2008

Though the stunned world of journalism was yet reeling from the sudden death of news media giant Tim Russert and many moving tributes flooded the television airwaves in solemn respect for a man who positively influenced so many people, the news media did not take a hiatus from spin driven reporting. Surprisingly, on the morning broadcast of MSNBC's "Morning Joe" with host Joe Scarborough, a few moments were taken by him, his co-host, and guest panel members to reflect favorably on Hillary Clinton and her campaign efforts for the Democratic Party nomination for the Presidency. Comments were made about how hard she fought for women and all Americans during the challenging days of the primary contests, and about her becoming "more human" and seemingly less detached, even more-so than Senator Barack Obama. It was, however, unfortunate that such positive things that could have been said about her during the Democratic primaries were strategically held in reserve until Senator Obama was presumed to have clinched the party nomination. Now the comments made by agents of the news media in her defense seemed disingenuous and smacked of bold faced hypocrisy. The same type of praise was heaped upon Clinton the following day when a panel of political strategists joined Chris Matthews on his broadcast of MSNBC's "Hardball with Chris Matthews." Matthews displayed the latest cover of *New York Magazine* which had a larger than life head shot of a glowing Hillary Clinton with the word "Superstar" stamped on the bottom right corner. Each of the panel members then offered his or her form of praise for the very same candidate that many news media outlets to include this one actively campaigned against during the Democratic Party primaries through lopsided coverage, stinging innuendos, and tasteless jokes about pantsuits. I wondered where this magazine cover was when *Time* magazine printed a similar cover with a headshot of a smiling Senator Obama with the words "and the winner is......." printed beneath. It is doubtful that the good folks at *New York Magazine* would have had the gonadic fortitude to print such a cover when Obama and Clinton were in a dead heat for the Democratic Party nomination, going against the news media party line of overwhelmingly negative press coverage for Clinton and the opposite for Obama. It is even more doubtful that Chris Matthews and the good folks at MSNBC would have dared to display such a cover on any of the network's programs if printed prior to Senator Obama becoming the Democratic Party presumptive nominee, or uttered a word about Clinton that could even remotely be taken as an indication of balance in their reporting during the primary elections.

During the Democratic and Republican Party primary elections, news media correspondents and networks alike never missed an opportunity to label candidates as flip floppers when they changed sides in support of or not to support issues ranging from the war in Iraq to drilling on protected lands to curb the cost of gas at the pump. While the American people have witnessed many extreme and clear cut cases of flip flopping in American politics, the Media Political Machine was now guilty of one of the most blatant cases of flip flopping ever committed by any political figure or entity and there were videos and transcripts to tell the story both truthfully and in its entirety of how agents of the American news media sacked Clinton's campaign in 2008 for the Democratic nomination through toxic, lopsided reporting and were now pretending to be her biggest advocates and supporters.

27 June 2008

CNN aired a story titled, "The Obama Look,"[46] about a designer clothing line being introduced by world renowned Italian designer, Donatella Versace which she said was inspired by Obama. Donatella was interviewed by a CNN correspondent and said that she was stirred to introduce the clothing line by Senator Obama's message of "change." During an interview for the story, Versace stated in regards to Obama: "I said wow, this is a man that I would like to inspire me for this collection because he is all about change and hope and, you know, challenge of the future."[47] The same story ended with a jab at Senator McCain when Versace commented that, style-wise, Senator McCain was "too constrictive" and that he "should loosen up a bit."[48] The story was perceptibly a stretch in regards to being politically relevant to any issue surrounding the upcoming Democrat and Republican National Conventions, the General Election, or issues important to American voters, however CNN once again succeeded in heaping more favorable press time on Senator Obama and making another dig at Senator McCain.

In the story immediately following the fashion news, CNN took another opportunity to raise the question as to what the future role of Senator Clinton would be in light of Senator Obama becoming the Democratic Party presumptive nominee for the presidency. Though the story started out as an attempt to convince viewers that Senator Clinton still *needed* Obama to both help dissolve her residual campaign debt and maintain her legacy in the Democratic Party, it quickly turned into being critical of former President Clinton. The network reported that according to a trusted but unnamed source, the former President was yet angry with the results of the Democratic primary elections race, and how, in his opinion, the Barack Obama campaign for the presidency was in some regards an anti-Clinton campaign. It was also said that the former President felt that the Obama campaign went out of its way to portray him as being a racist during the campaign. A representative from *Time* magazine was interviewed to lend credibility to the story that was the latest edition in a series of stories aired by the network, painting the former President in a tremendously negative light. The representative from the magazine willingly played into the intent of the story through making the statement that the former President was bitter about Senator Clinton's defeat and should support Senator Obama as the Democratic nominee for the presidency or get on with the work of his foundation. Ironically, the former President did just that almost immediately after Senator Clinton's concession speech after her defeat, yet he was criticized for not doing more to reach out in support of Senator Obama. The *Time* magazine representative also commented that he was "surprised by the way the former President was acting" following the Democratic primaries—after all, why should former President Clinton be mad about being portrayed by the news media as a racist when he built a lifelong legacy for being a champion for supporting and uplifting minorities, spanning throughout his days as President and extending throughout his days as a former President. According to the sentiments of the "most trusted" news network, the former President should have ignored the smear campaign against him and Senator Clinton led by the news media and joined them in efforts to crown Senator Obama as the great hope of American society fed up with eight years of a failed Republican administration.

The media obsession with the every move of former President Clinton seemed to intensify as news correspondents found themselves playing Where's Waldo in regards to his whereabouts during a campaign rally in a town named Unity, in which Senators Obama and Clinton appeared together on the same stage for the common cause of unifying the Democratic Party supporters for Senator Obama's nomination for the presidency. Many correspondents such as CNN's Candy Crowley, who rose to prominence in news reporting as a covert advocate for the Bush Administration while serving as a CNN White House correspondent, were now providing viewers with commentary regarding what the absence of the former President from the event meant and why he should support Senator Obama's bid for the presidency. This was the tune now despite the news media being the harshest of his critics while he blazed the trails in support of Senator Clinton's campaign for the very same purpose. Yet another case of flip flopping was revealed when the same media correspondents and networks who labeled Bill Clinton as a liability to Senator Clinton's campaign, arguably due to fear that he would help catapult her to the nomination victory she so diligently sought, and insinuated that he was a racist, now had the audacity to insist upon his presence at Obama campaign rallies. Could it be that the Media Political Machine did not want Bill Clinton to somehow pull off another victory for the Clinton legacy in American politics through campaigning unfettered for Senator Clinton, but now wanted to convince viewers of what a tremendous asset he would be campaigning for Senator Obama? This certainly seemed to be the case and the latest in a series of acts of hypocrisy and flip flops on the part of the spin driven Media Political Machine which were intended to go undetected by news media network viewers. What was more is the fact that since none of the news media networks or correspondents were playing Where's Waldo with other past Presidents and prominent political figures in regards to the support of the two presumptive nominees for the presidency, it was obvious that the inquisition was nothing more than the latest in an unwavering attack on the former President's character and legacy. If this was not the case, then questions should have been raised as to the whereabouts of former Presidents Jimmy Carter, George H.W. Bush, current President George W. Bush, and former First Lady, Nancy Reagan during the Obama and McCain campaign rallies just as was the case with former President Clinton. Instead, several news media television networks were now attempting to strong arm the former President into campaigning for Senator Obama by stating that, again, "unnamed sources" close to Bill Clinton had revealed to them that he was "angry with Obama" regarding attacks regarding his character during the Democratic primaries. This was the case even though, only months prior, Clinton was repeatedly referred to as a political liability to the Hillary Clinton campaign for the presidency. This led to the question, if the former President was considered such a major risk to the campaign of his own wife, then how on earth could he now be an asset to Senator Obama's bid for the presidency?

30 June 2008

The CBS News online homepage featured a story written by Ben Smith of Politico.com following comments made by former NATO Supreme Allied Commander, Retired General Wesley Clark, to CBS veteran correspondent Bob Schieffer after being asked a question in regards to the relevance of Senator John McCain's military service to his being qualified to serve as the nation's President.[49] Though Clark did not characterize McCain's service, Smith's story brought to light criticism by some Obama supporters that suggested Senator McCain's military service was not all that honorable due to his taking part in a propaganda video as a prisoner of war in Vietnam, despite being his being tortured and coerced into doing so. One source cited in the CBS story, Doug Valentine of *Counterpunch*, the "bi-weekly muckraking liberal newsletter" edited by Alexander Cockburn and Jeffery St. Clair, went as far as to state that Senator McCain was a "war criminal" who bombed innocent civilians as a Navy pilot, invoking memories of right-wing attacks on the military service record of Senator John Kerry during the 2004 presidential election.[50] Valentine's highly controversial story that leveled both strong and highly negative accusations at McCain in regards to his military service was titled, "From Glory Boy to PW Songbird, John McCain: War Hero or North Vietnam's Go-To Collaborator?"[51]

After navigating to the Politico.com Website, I found, upon closer inspection, that Smith injected very little of his own opinion into his piece, instead citing several opinions complete with sources, yielding a fairly balanced account of questions surrounding McCain's military service. Smith's story was objectively titled: "Some On Left Target McCain's War Record," and lacked the element of smear found throughout the story by Valentine. After reading several other stories on the Politico Website, I found stories that both supported Senator Obama as an agent for change as well as criticized him for failing to take decisive stands regarding issues that could polarize him from one block of voters or another. This approach to news reporting contrasted sharply with many television news programs by presenting factual information coupled with opinions from outside sources that were cited by name in most cases instead of simply stating, "an unnamed source said..........," which leaves the door open for the insertion of outright lies in news reporting to distort and persuade viewers to think a certain way about a given issue. Even the Websites of leading news networks revealed bias not found at Politico, at the time, through the choice to post certain types of stories that leaned in one direction or the other with little if any opposing viewpoints other than those fabricated for dishonorable reasons. A prime example of this was CBS citing the Valentine story which was highly critical of Senator McCain's military service record and read more like a tabloid article along with that of Ben Smith who painted a more balanced piece about the same subject while advancing the idea of taking a closer look at McCain's service record.

2 July 2008

As the gradual dying down of political rhetoric became apparent during CNN's evening broadcasts, it was also apparent that the intensity of their bias had toned down dramatically with the elimination of Senator Hillary Clinton as a contender for the Democratic Party nomination for the presidency. With every broadcast, the softening of the network's toxic tone and the absence of some of its most opinionative and biased correspondents made it unmistakably apparent that the sharpest criticism and bias they so readily laced news stories with about which they reported in the months prior, was driven by a hidden agenda aimed squarely at Senator Clinton and former President Clinton as they campaigned for Senator Clinton's claim to the Democratic Party nomination.

The evening broadcast of Election Center with Campbell Brown who wielded some of the sharpest criticism against the Hillary Clinton campaign for the presidency was graced by the unbiased and pleasant reporting of correspondent Soledad O'Brien who hosted the show in Brown's absence. O'Brien succeeded, though temporarily, in restoring dignity and respectability to the broadcast by remaining neutral in her delivery and questioning of guests and panel members. She respectfully covered the latest stories on Senator's Obama and McCain in a manner that was not insulting to the intelligence of her viewers though much of the broadcast focused on the release of fifteen hostages held by a Columbian militant group.

The balance and lack of bias O'Brien displayed during her delivery revealed that perhaps the network allowed its correspondents the latitude to freely inject their own personal views and bias into the news they reported, and that it is just as much the fault of the correspondents for choosing to report news in a toxic manner as it is that of the network which employs them for allowing it.

4 July 2008

The Independence Day broadcast of Headline News brought a surprising inconsistency in the network's manner of news reporting that had been historically marked by brevity regarding the amount of time devoted to each story and few cases of toxic reporting. Around 7:30 a.m., the network aired a story focused on inconsistencies in Senator Barack Obama's position on ending the war in Iraq. When Senator Obama began his campaign months earlier, he made statements to voters that upon being elected President, he would end the war in Iraq and withdraw American troops only months after taking office. His stand on 4 July, regarding the controversial issue, was to, upon being elected, listen to the commanders on the ground and withdraw troops in a calculated and responsible manner that would allow for the Iraqi government to maintain control of the country following the exit of U.S. Soldiers. This was such a drastic change in Senator Obama's previous position that he was prompted to give two speeches clarifying his stand on the issue. While Headline News correctly, by current definition, referred to this as an extreme case of political flip flopping, the network seemed to go out of its way to downplay the issue for Obama by introducing a poll which asked voters which candidate, McCain or Obama, was most inconsistent when confronting the political issues that mattered most to them. The result was 59% for Senator Obama and 61% for Senator McCain which was a virtual tie due to the margin of error allowed. The spin that the correspondent and guest correspondent for the broadcast placed on the issue was that due to the magnitude and multitude of the adverse issues that the American public currently faced, with the failing economy, rising gas prices and the war in Iraq and Afghanistan, the act of political flip flopping was not as much of an issue to American voters as in elections past. This marked another clear inconsistency on the part of the Media Political Machine which, up to this point, had always reported flip flopping on the part of politicians as a most serious negative act with which voters should be concerned. This was the case, most recently, in the case of Senator McCain's many noted inconsistencies regarding stands he had taken on several issues prior to the primary election campaigns versus during. Only a few short years prior, Senator and Presidential hopeful John Kerry was crucified by the Republican Party and the media for noted flip flops during and prior to his presidential campaign. Now that Senator Obama, who the media seemed to favor during the 2008 election season, was noted to have flip flopped on an issue, the same media sought to convince viewers that flip flopping was now OK, which, in turn was, ironically, another flip flop on the part of the Media Political Machine.

20 July 2008

On this day it seemed that one of the "most trusted" news stations somehow stumbled up on the revelation that Senator Obama, at the time out of the country visiting Middle Eastern nations to shore up his foreign relations experience, was receiving the lion's share of the press coverage leading up to the Democrat and Republican National Conventions while Senator John McCain could barely scare up an honorable mention. The standard payroll panel was called in to analyze the issue and explain away why coverage of two presidential hopefuls had been so lopsided. None of the arguments as to why this was occurring amounted to much more than Senator Obama just happened to be a more fascinating candidate than old boring what's his name. As the story continued to unfold, however, and with the mention of rival network CBS News having sent three anchors, including Katie Couric, to the Middle East with Senator Obama to provide exclusive coverage of the campaign trip, it became obvious that the story was nothing more than sour grapes on the part of CNN because CBS News was covering the trip exclusively instead of other more "trusted" networks. The hypocrisy was almost unbearable at the point when the news correspondent moderating the finger pointing program had the gall to hold up five recent copies of *Newsweek* magazine with Senator Obama, splashed larger than life, on the cover of each one, as if his own network was not guilty of overwhelmingly lopsided coverage, spanning the course of the campaign season. It was doubtful that the raising of this issue, though in dire need of being addressed, was in the interest of the network's viewers or the nation's voters. If this was the case, then the most serious, trusted, fair and balanced of the offended news entities could have simply led the charge and stopped the biased coverage and spin driven reporting cold turkey. It was most likely, however, the Media Political Machine sought to send Senator Obama a covert message that the most prominent entities of the news media had the power to turn off the overwhelming favorable coverage he enjoyed during the majority of his campaign whenever it chose to. It was all too apparent that CNN and other news media entities crying foul at the time were driven once again by self interest and were upset that Senator Obama went to the prom with anther network after all they did for him thus far during the '08 election season.

21 July 2008

As predictable as the sunrise, following Senator Obama's snub of some of the leading news media outlets by giving CBS correspondents exclusive access to him during his Middle East campaign tour, within hours, the Media Political Machine turned on him like an Egyptian cobra. Several evening news broadcasts raised the issue regarding Senator Obama getting far greater media coverage than Senator McCain. CNN presented poll results that 73% believed that the media was sharply biased in favor of Obama. One of Obama's most devoted self-appointed media cheerleaders during the intense campaign contest with Hillary Clinton, correspondent Campbell Brown, led a discussion complete with a payroll panel regarding the *New York Times'* rejection of an op ed piece written by Senator McCain as a rebuttal to an article they published previously by Senator Obama, outlining his plan for the war in Iraq. Brown was now, however sowing seeds of doubt and deceit about Obama's integrity with the introduction of this issue as well as another in which she made reference to his Middle East campaign trip, being paid for by taxpayer dollars, while conveniently failing to remind viewers that Obama was yet a U.S. Senator. Right wing sympathizer Candy Crowley also chimed in following an up to the day re-cap of the Obama Mid-East trip, that though Obama seemed to be benefiting in the polls from his trip, there were yet pitfalls that he should look out for, as if she was ominously predicting him to make a political misstep. Campbell Brown then asked Crowley if Obama's brief trip to the region would really do much for the foreign relations section of his resume, setting the stage for more negative dialogue regarding Obama. The introduction of another poll was made regarding which candidate was more prepared to be Commander in Chief, Senator Obama or Senator McCain. On this night, McCain conveniently reigned supreme by receiving a 72% to 38% vote of confidence by those polled according to CNN.

Correspondent Dana Bash who often displayed favor for conservatives during reporting in the past, was now following Senator McCain around the campaign trail. She announced that religious right leader James Dobson was pondering throwing his support behind McCain, whom he once declared he would not support, because he now reportedly felt that Obama, as the alternative, would be a far worse choice.

During a behind the scenes "stagecraft" critical analysis of Obama's Middle East trip, it was pointed out that many pictures were taken and footage shot of Obama with military leaders and Soldiers, because "he never served in uniform," and did not support the surge of military personnel in Iraq to quell the violence and re-institute stability in the war torn nation. Following several more instances of the obvious media assault on Obama that evening which was a carryover because of his choice to favor CBS for coverage over other media outlets during his trip, outspoken correspondent Glenn Beck, conveniently stood in for Larry King on the "Larry King Live" show to re-heat the leftovers regarding the issue of the media's overwhelming press coverage of the Obama campaign of which the network that employed him, at the time, was also party to. Beck proceeded to rake Obama over the coals regarding his not supporting the troop surge in Iraq, stating Obama made a "colossal error in judgment--something that he seems a little prone to."[52] This statement marked another flip flop on the part of the Media Political Machine that would not have uttered such words about Obama on this particular network while he was yet campaigning to defeat Senator Clinton for the Democratic nomination. Beck went on to state that American citizens were "screaming out for change," and "not getting it from either candidate," covertly dismissing Obama, by playing on the words of his own campaign slogan, as just another politician.[53] Following Beck's "Larry King Live" appearance, Anderson Cooper joined the dog pile by stating that Obama may have overstepped his boundary as a presidential hopeful by issuing a statement that the Iraqi Prime Minister agreed with his sixteen month time table for a troop withdrawal from Iraq. No statement regarding Cooper's assumption was issued by the White House or the Secretary of State. The most compelling evidence of the Media Political Machine's attempt to send a message to Senator Obama that it could make or break him with the airing of a broadcast or the printing of a story was the obvious surge in the amount of positive press time given to Senator McCain during the evening broadcasts on more than one news station that gave him more coverage in a single night than he had received in the entire preceding six months combined from most networks. The unanimous message of the evening from the news media to the Obama campaign seemed to be: if you snub us by not allowing the rest of us a portion of the access to your campaign activities again, we will ensure your campaign goes the way of Senator Clinton's at our hands during the primary elections.

30 July 2008

After the wounds were healed following Senator Obama's snub of many media outlets during his trip to the Middle East, it was business as usual for the Media Political Machine. While stories produced by the machine favorably focusing on the McCain campaign for the presidency in 2008 continued to be scarce as hen teeth, and while correspondents like Campbell Brown overemphasized Senator McCain's age in comparison to that of past presidential candidates with the exception of President Ronald Reagan, the *New York Times* and other appendages of the machine published articles touting Senator Obama as an exceptional college professor during his previous occupation as an educator. In a story titled "Teaching Law, Testing Ideas, Obama Stood Slightly Apart,"[54] a story written by Jodi Kantor, the author, using factual, referenced information, described Obama in his days as a college professor, as a "thoughtful listener and questioner" who honed many of his ideas and political ideology in the classes he taught at the University of Chicago Law School. In the lengthy, but insightful article, Kantor covered Senator Obama's years as Senior Lecturer at the school, highlighting things from Obama's professional relationship with his students to lectures he gave regarding the issue of segregation. The story also touched on Obama's knack for often not taking a decisive stand on issues that could affect him in an adverse manner, politically in the future, which was a point the news media often avoided, instead opting to extensively cover issues irrelevant to the presidential race such as Senator McCain's latest skin biopsy and whether or not it would test positive for melanoma.

While Kantor's story did show some semblances of balance in regards to triumphs and setbacks Senator Obama experienced as a young professor, attempting to break into state and national politics, the overall content of the story was, once again, overwhelmingly favorable for Senator Obama.

There is absolutely nothing wrong with this manner of factual reporting as the lack of the author's spin driven opinion prevented the story from taking on toxic overtones. Where the problem lies, however, is the intentional restraint the news media exercised when covering positive aspects of other presidential hopefuls during the '08 elections. Few if any stories were published regarding Senator Clinton's life as a young attorney prior to her emergence onto the American political scene. The same was the case for Senator McCain as a young Navy pilot as well as for other presidential hopefuls who received virtually no news media coverage during their campaigns. This overt practice by the news media during the 2008 election season introduced toxicity into campaign coverage, affording an unfair advantage to one candidate over all others.

4 August 2008

Just as viewers began to think the seemingly endless assault by the media on Senator and former President Clinton was over due to her departure from the race for the Democratic Party nomination for the presidency, CNN rolled out the payroll panel on the Situation Room with Wolf Blitzer yet again. Following the suggestion by David Gergen, one of the network's leading political contributor's suggestion that Senator Obama should reconsider choosing Senator Clinton as a vice presidential running mate due to a lackluster performance by the Democratic presumptive nominee against Senator John McCain in the polls at the time. The very same network that sang her praises when she bowed out of the race after pummeling her in almost every broadcast during the election season, was now once again rallying members of the media's anti-Clinton crusade against her because to some it was beginning to look like Senator Obama might be inclined to bring her aboard for the number two position after all. The argument made by the panel members including CNN Senior Political Analyst, Gloria Borger and a random Republican strategist was, of course, that Senator Clinton would not bring Senator Obama's campaign a boost in the polls though Clinton's supporters numbering in excess of 18 million voters would give Obama's campaign a very much needed shot in the arm to break the 50% approval polling mark over Senator McCain. This move by network correspondents and contributors seemed to give credence to the observation that the support of the Obama campaign by the Media Political Machine was not so much pro-Obama as it was anti-Clinton. The Republican strategist, when asked by Blitzer how the Republican Party would feel about Senator Clinton being named as Senator Obama's running mate for the General Election, responded that the party would be "ecstatic" about it because it would secure a Republican victory in November. Of course, because the words were those of a GOP strategist, and he was a member of a CNN panel, it was more likely this was nothing more than rhetoric to keep viewers from coming to the realization that Republicans were terrified at the idea of Clinton being named to round out the ticket because they were 0 and 3, counting Senator Clinton's election to the U.S. Senate, against the so-called Clinton Political Machine.

Later in the evening, news media Clinton basher Campbell Brown initiated the lowest form of toxic reporting through facilitating a discussion complete with payroll panel regulars, and self appointed Obama campaign media drum major, Roland Martin who spouted several untruths during the broadcast regarding the former President's African American base abandoning him entirely. Martin went as far as to make the left field statement that Bill Clinton "loved being in black churches" and "he can't go in those now,"[55] which was totally untrue, but typical of puppets of the Media Political Machine who simply made up news when the conveyance of facts did not fit their agenda. Campbell Brown then interjected, quite insolently as had become her trademark, the snide remark that Senator Clinton should tell the former President to "shut up"[56] during the remaining days of her political campaign.

This was not the first time Brown had displayed her perceived contempt for former President Clinton and acute un-professionalism when reporting stories regarding him in an overly biased manner. It was also not the first time she exponentially elevated the level of toxicity in news reporting while simultaneously taking her network to a new low in regards to serious and "trusted" news reporting. – So much for her latest broadcast slogan, "No Bias, No Bull."

If hypocrisy was a crime, some of the correspondents employed by CNN and many other leading news media networks would draw immediate life sentences. On the evening broadcast of Larry King Live, Larry King interviewed quick witted and sharp minded billionaire T. Boone Pickens along with Sir Richard Branson and others regarding the answer to the current and projected energy crisis in the United States. At one point during the interview, King pointed out that Pickens was, at the time, 80 years of age. The ironic thing about this was the fact that the same network that repeatedly made it a well documented point to reference Senator John McCain's age in a negative manner in regards to fitness to serve as President was now flip flopping on its seemingly age discriminating platform by interviewing a highly successful "senior" regarding national and world energy issues. Such hypocrisy made it increasingly harder by the day to continue to regard the network as even *one of* the "most trusted" names in news reporting.

7 August 2008

On the evening of 7 August 2008, the broadcast of CNN's Anderson Cooper 360 stirred more controversy regarding Senator Hillary Clinton and the eighteen million voters who supported her during the primary elections. Host Anderson Cooper backed by correspondent Candy Crowley succeeded in stirring the rumor mill with a very brief video clip of Clinton speaking to a group of seemingly frustrated female supporters at an unnamed gathering. A clip of former President Clinton was also played during which he answered a question regarding whether Senator Obama was "ready" to be President. Since the former President did not answer the question in the manner which the news media thought he should have responded, he was criticized during the broadcast, and the statement was made by a correspondent that "a simple yes or no" answer would have sufficed.

Following the show opening rhetoric regarding the Clinton effect on the Obama campaign, stemming from the news media's sentiments that both Senator Clinton and former President Clinton were not as engaged as they should have been in supporting Senator Obama on the campaign trail, the focus turned strangely to the former President and what the media said was a perceived bitterness on the part of him as a result of Senator Clinton losing her party nomination bid. After several clips of Clinton speaking candidly to an ABC News reporter, however, it was obvious that his displeasure was largely with the countless cases of the news media's abhorrently biased coverage of the primary elections and the smear campaign it waged against both Clintons rather than with Senator Obama's victory. Correspondent Candy Crowley, who was often embedded with the Hillary Clinton campaign during the primary elections, then spoke at length with Anderson Cooper about the Clintons "needing to do more" to show their support for Senator Obama which was highly hypocritical because of repeated statements made by CNN correspondents as well as those from other networks that both Clinton's were a liability to the Democratic bid to regain the

White House. Crowley then injected more toxicity into the story by stating "conspiracy theorists," who of course remained unnamed, believed the Clintons were not doing more to support Senator Obama's campaign because they wanted him to lose to make way for a possible future run for Senator Clinton in four years.[57] This was of course mere speculation, because nobody actually heard either of the Clintons make statements confirming the existence of ill intended motives for use against Obama. The negativity of the statement regarding the Clintons alleged intentions during the broadcast fanned the flames of toxicity and alluded to the Clintons orchestrating a clandestine campaign to undermine Obama. What was ironic was the fact that while agents of the Media Political Machine could never quite put their finger on the existence of a clandestine campaign within the news media to destroy all political campaigns counter to the Obama campaign, they were quite adept at detecting the existence of clandestine campaigns that sought to derail the Obama campaign.

At this point in the campaign season, it was also apparent that the Media Political Machine was changing its position regarding the Clintons in that it was ok for the them to support Obama for the presidency unbridled, though it was not acceptable for the former President to mount the stump for his wife during the life cycle of her campaign. If the Clintons needed to do more to support Senator Obama in his bid for the presidency, baggage in tow, then why was the news media not requiring the same of President George W. Bush and Vice President Dick Cheney in support of Senator McCain's campaign?

11 August 2008

The September 2008 edition of *The Atlantic* magazine, volume 302, number 2, featured a story titled "The Front-Runner's Fall."[58] Though the magazine had a date of September, it arrived on the newsstands in August just days before the anticipated announcement by Senator Obama regarding who would be his choice of a vice presidential running mate for the General Election. The story was written by magazine journalist Joshua Green and focused upon what he described as the "epic collapse" of the Hillary Clinton campaign for the presidency in 2008. The story was unprecedented in a sense that never before had a campaign been so scrutinized and criticized for failing to succeed. The story's release was moreover timed perfectly so as to inject toxicity into the election process through releasing insider's information regarding strategies that were considered for use against the Obama campaign at a time when Clinton could have still been considered by Obama for the number two spot on the Democratic ticket. Quotes contained in Green's story were certain to make the Obama campaign skeptical of bringing Clinton on board with the leak of such close hold information that revealed lines of attack for use against Obama during the height of the Democratic primary elections. Quotes published by the magazine included the following statements made by Clinton campaign pollster and strategist Mark Penn regarding Obama: "All of these articles about his boyhood in Indonesia and his life in Hawaii are geared towards showing his background is diverse, multicultural and putting that in new light. Save it for 2050.—It also exposes a very strong weakness for him—his roots to basic American values and culture are at best limited. I cannot imagine America electing a president during a time of war who is not at his center fundamentally American in his thinking and in his values."[59] Statements such as these obviously did Hillary Clinton no favors as a possible contender for the number two spot on the Democratic ticket and reflected the fact that opportunists in the ranks of her campaign failed to read "Stickin',"[60] a book written by one of her strongest supporters, James Carville, regarding the importance of loyalty in politics. Unfortunately, the news media was able to prey on this disloyalty to obtain information that it used in news media broadcasts and publications so as to render Senator Clinton's consideration for the number two spot on the Obama ticket a questionable move.

The main idea of the story seemed to be an in-depth look at the Clinton campaign for the purpose of focusing on infighting among key staffers and alleged indecision on the part of Clinton herself as the final authority of the campaign. This was most likely the case with every other unsuccessful presidential campaign of 2008, however, Clinton's was, quite ironically, the only one chosen for dissection. In addition to Green highlighting these campaign issues, he also mentioned Clinton's struggles with the news media, though in a manner that made it seem as though her campaign had difficulties with the media due to being disorganized, forcing Clinton to rely on the news media to dog pile Senator Obama at some point during the primary elections to reverse her campaign's negative image, which the news media, of course, was careful to never do. Green failed to spend any time focusing on the difference in the type of media coverage Clinton received during the campaign versus that of Obama, easily letting the news media off the hook for its surreptitious transgressions of overtly biased coverage. The remainder of the story was more of the same from the Media Political Machine, outlining all the reasons for the failure of the Clinton for President campaign of 2008 with the exception of the role the news media played in running a campaign counter to Clinton's at the same time she battled Obama's popular campaign for change.

16 August 2008

On the evening of 16 August, a town hall meeting styled forum was held in California, marking the first time Senators John McCain and Barack Obama attended any semblance of a debate together as presumptive nominees of their respective political parties for the presidency. The forum was hosted by Pastor Rick Warren and held at the Saddleback Church in Orange County, California. The forum proved to be the most balanced and impartial question and answer session involving more than one candidate for the presidency, arguably due to the fact the Media Political Machine was not the sponsor of and did not supply the moderator for the forum. Though the forum took place in its entirety without a hitch and remained unbiased and impartial through both candidates being asked the exact same questions, free from rhetoric, by neutral host Warren, the day following the forum's broadcast, CNN's correspondent Rick Sanchez found fault with it while interviewing Warren regarding the forum on the afternoon news broadcast. Sanchez suggestively questioned Warren regarding a statement he made that Senator McCain was located in a "cone of silence" during Senator Obama's question and answer session which took place before that of Senator McCain following a pre-forum coin toss that awarded the first hour to Obama. Warren, on the night of the forum, referred to McCain being in a cone of silence to assure viewers that the veteran senator was located somewhere in which he could not hear or view the forum during Senator Obama's Q and A session. Sanchez made the revelation while interviewing Pastor Warren that he had information that confirmed Senator McCain was not actually in the building at the time Warren made the statement and was instead in route to the Saddleback Church even as Senator Obama was participating in his hour of the forum. Sanchez then went on the offensive, quizzing Pastor Warren about his statement and whether or not he was aware McCain was not in the building at the time he made it. Sanchez also asked Warren how he could be sure that McCain was not somewhere viewing or listening to the broadcast while Senator Obama was being interviewed, bringing the integrity of Warren and McCain into question and insinuating Senator Obama was possibly at a disadvantage by being interviewed by the pastor first. Sanchez also kept with the network tradition of attacking candidates that opposed Senator Obama by making reference to a statement McCain made during his hour of the interview in which he was asked to define what he considered to be wealthy. Sanchez paraphrased McCain's answer that a person making roughly five million dollars in income per year was wealthy in his view. Sanchez then made a statement and facial gesture insinuating that Senator McCain's answer was an indication that he was out of touch and possibly elitist in his view. Sanchez made no such effort to bring into question any of Senator Obama's actions or answers from the night of the forum during the broadcast.

18 August 2008

CNN's Jack Cafferty wrote an opinionative piece on the CNN Website Blog Archive section regarding the cone of silence controversy, seemingly performing damage control for the network and Media Political Machine, because it was apparent that viewers were beginning to pull back the curtain on the wizard, and the media was being exposed for its inimitably biased coverage during the campaign season. The often crass and controversial Cafferty, in his brief blog entry, referred to Senator McCain as a "whiner" and proceeded to take up for NBC's Andrea Mitchell who was criticized by some for bringing the issue up on "Meet the Press." Cafferty was also critical of McCain's campaign manager, Rick Davis for, reportedly, requesting to meet with the president of NBC News regarding, not surprisingly, biased news reporting by the network. Cafferty's words reeked of contempt for McCain and were a very thinly veiled attempt to again bring into question Senator McCain's integrity regarding the issue triggered by the McCain campaign's questioning the obvious abandoning of non-partisan coverage by the news media. Cafferty closed his commentary with the typical media reply to the questioning of its integrity regarding balanced coverage during the campaigns—the statistic. He then presented results of a "media study" that came out a month prior, finding that ABC, CBS, and NBC were tougher on Senator Obama than McCain during the "first six weeks" of the general election campaign.

It was not at all surprising that Cafferty was so protective of the exposure of Media Political Machine's toxic reporting tactics. After all, it had protected him during his time of controversy and swept his own recent verbal folly under the rug, limiting coverage of a lawsuit filed against him on behalf of the citizens of the Republic of China. On the April 9th broadcast of CNN's Situation Room, Cafferty, during one of his overdramatic rants regarding both lead contaminated and faulty Chinese imports, made the following statements: "So I think our relationship with China has certainly changed. I think they're basically the same bunch of goons and thugs they've been for the last 50 years."[61] Cafferty's comments set off a firestorm of controversy between him and Chinese citizens who held that it reflected his hostility toward the citizens of China and his unbridled bias during the broadcast of a serious politically charged network program. To add insult to injury, the network and the Media Political Machine stood by their man, ensuring the coverage of the controversy was limited, and commenting that he was no more biased against the citizens of China than he was against all others he chose to openly spout contempt for in publications and during network broadcasts. It was unfortunate that some recent contenders of the 2008 primary elections were not afforded a second chance by the news media after a political slip up as was Cafferty and choice others.

20 August 2008

Much ado regarding Senator Barack Obama's pending announcement of who was to be his vice-presidential running mate the week leading up to the Democratic National Convention in Denver, Colorado overshadowed another notable story of national importance. Ohio Congresswoman Stephanie Tubbs Jones, a fifth term Democrat from Cleveland Heights, and the chairman of the House Ethics Committee in the United States House of Representatives died suddenly of an aneurysm after a full day of activities, only a day prior, in her home district. Even after Senator Obama missed the Wednesday announcement deadline set by the Media Political Machine for his VP pick, leading television news networks spent more time speculating and strategizing regarding who Obama would select than memorializing a pillar of the nation's government, an outspoken advocate of the people, and a Democratic National Party superdelegate.

If Representative Stephanie Tubbs Jones was more than simply the first black woman to represent the people of Ohio in the House of Representatives, a loyal friend and unyielding supporter of democracy, a seasoned speaker and stateswoman, and one of the few who dared to be bold enough to say no to a resolution supporting the presence of American troops in Iraq because it went against her better judgment, maybe the news media would have afforded her more than a terse honorable mention on prime time broadcasts in the days following her death. Even on news media Websites, the story of Tubbs Jones' death was not worthy of the "breaking news" label used so commonly during the election season to announce the latest attempt to smear candidates opposing the media's choice for the presidency. At best, the news of Tubbs Jones' untimely death was listed as the fourth or fifth bullet on news media Websites under "latest news." Unfortunately a yet unnamed vice-presidential candidate and the potential for an announcement regarding the revelation of who "got the call" from Senator Obama, to come at any moment, eclipsed the due respect for and memory of a woman who epitomized leadership at the highest level in our government. It appeared that in her deceased state, Tubbs Jones could do little for the ratings of the Media Political Machine, so she was no longer of any use to it. Did I mention Tubbs Jones was one of the staunchest supporters of Hillary Clinton during her campaign for the presidency in 2008?

22 August 2008

On the CNN Website under the politics section, the network shared the thoughts of one of its political commentators in a piece titled "Who gets second billing on the presidential ballot?"[62] The focus of the section was an opinion piece regarding what each potential vice presidential contender for both Senators John McCain and Barack Obama would bring to a respective running mate's campaign. Each contender was rated by the writer using a pro and con approach which listed one or two pros and a few more cons beside a file picture of each projected vice presidential hopeful. Some of those listed were very well known and others were more of a dark horse in nature. The section included evaluations of Senator Evan Bayh, Senator Joseph Biden, Retired General Wesley Clark, Senator Hillary Clinton, former Massachusetts Governor Mitt Romney, and former Arkansas Governor Mike Huckabee to name a few. What was interesting was the obvious personal bias that was apparent in only one of the narratives which rendered an otherwise well researched and informative piece regarding the vice presidential hopefuls, toxic in nature. Guess which one it was. Here are a few of the opinions listed by CNN regarding some of those considered by Senators Barack Obama and John McCain as potential vice presidential running mates. Notice the obvious personal attack in only one of the narratives which happens to be the same narrative in which the "pro" is marked by undeniable brevity and cynicism. In addition, it is easy to distinguish a difference in the tone of language used in the same narrative when compared to that of all other candidates listed under the section on the CNN Website. The narratives read as follows:

Mitt Romney
Age, Occupation
Pro: Romney, who founded the investment firm Bain Capital, brings a sterling business resume to a ticket headed by someone who once

joked that he was reading Alan Greenspan's book to learn about the economy.

Con: After a bitter primary campaign, can McCain and Romney really get along? The Democrats will remind voters of the nastiest barbs traded between McCain and Romney during the GOP primaries. Some social conservatives are turned off by Romney's religion. And no, Romney will not save the GOP ticket in liberal Massachusetts.[63]

Evan Bayh
Age, Occupation

Pro: Bayh's service on the Senate Intelligence and Armed Services committees would help shore up one of Obama's weak spots. Picking Bayh, a prominent Hillary Clinton surrogate, would help unite the Democrats after a lengthy primary. Running with this centrist Democrat would counter GOP arguments that Obama is a typical liberal and Indiana's 11 electoral votes wouldn't hurt either.

Con: Some liberals may have a hard time swallowing Bayh's support for a ban on partial-birth abortions. Also, because Bayh supported the war in Iraq, Obama may have a tough time defending his record after repeatedly emphasizing his own early opposition to the war.[64]

Hillary Clinton
Age, Occupation

Pro: There is no better way to unify the party than make the hero the running mate.

Con: Clinton is one of the *most divisive* politicians in America. Does Obama want to put such a *polarizing* figure on his ticket when he is trying to sell himself as someone who will turn the page on the partisan bickering? And does Obama *really think he'll be able to control Hillary—and Bill Clinton*—if he wins the White House?[65]

Michael Bloomberg
Age, Occupation

Pro: Tapping independent Bloomberg would send an extremely powerful message to moderate voters that McCain is still a maverick.

Con: The GOP may splinter. Picking the socially liberal Bloomberg would be the last straw for a lot of conservatives who have never warmed to the McCain campaign. Bloomberg almost certainly won't be able to save McCain in New York. And don't look for the 66 year old mayor to supply that dose of youth and vigor the McCain campaign is desperately looking for.[66]

In addition to the obvious bias found on the CNN Website regarding potential Vice Presidential candidates, top stories on the AT&T Yahoo webpage for the same date reflected story titles with a clear bias in favor of one presumptive nominee over the other. The following stories were listed on the site as the day's top news stories:
--A housing issue: McCain not sure how many they own (AP)
--Obama inspires black Republicans to switch parties (AP)
--Campaigns vie over whether McCain is a Bush clone (AP)
--Obama casts McCain as rich, out of touch (AP)
--Veep Sheet: Obama meets Kaine's staff (Politico)

30 August 2008

On the day following Senator John McCain's announcement that dark horse and Washington outsider, Alaska former Governor Sarah Palin was his pick for the vice presidency leading up to the Republican National Convention, the news media initiated a subtle assault against him for his decision that was sure to gain momentum in the days to come. Headline News aired a story titled, "McCain's Calculated Move," focused on Senator McCain's recent announcement of his choice for a running mate for his party's nomination for Vice President. Headline News Correspondent Ed Henry delivered the story in a manner that subtly questioned Senator McCain's judgment in selecting his choice for VP and then Governor Palin's qualification for the number two spot on the Republican ticket. During the broadcast of the story, Henry and a lead correspondent attempted to covertly impress doubt upon program viewers using the presence of a caption located at the bottom of the screen that read, "McCain's Gamble." The correspondents also introduced negative points of view regarding issue without claiming responsibility through using lead-in phrases such as, "some observers say," and by referring to McCain's selection of Palin as a "calculated move" to attract so-called disgruntled Hillary Clinton supporters.

In addition to copious statements with negative undertones, easily detectable by program viewers, regarding this issue, a negatively charged statement issued by an Obama campaign spokesman which questioned whether Palin was qualified to serve as Vice President of the U.S., being only "a heartbeat away" from the nation's highest office was underscored. The heartbeat away reference regurgitated by the correspondents several times during the brief story both alluded, once again, to the news media's issue with Senator McCain's age, and to former Governor Palin's preparedness for elevation to the office of President in the event of Senator McCain's inability to complete a term.[67] Henry also made sure to point out that Palin was "far less" qualified than Senator Hillary Clinton to serve in the number two position. This marked the latest contradiction in reporting by the Media Political Machine which transcripts and historical footage will show, with the help of networks CNN, MSNBC, and numerous periodicals as well as printed media sources, questioned the qualifications of Senator Clinton to serve as President, citing her work as First Lady during the tenure of former President Clinton's Presidency could not be counted as "real experience." It seemed now, however, the news media saw fit, with Senator Clinton safely out of the race for either of her party's nominations for the '08 General Election, to use her credentials unfairly against former Governor Palin. These were the same credentials that the news media insisted were non-existent when Senator Clinton was vying for the Democratic National Party presidential nomination.

Other points highlighted during the broadcast which underscored preliminary efforts by the news media to put a negative spin on the Palin story instead of merely reporting factual information, included the statement that the former governor would not attract Hillary Clinton supporters due to her anti-abortion and other conservative stances. The statement was also made that Palin's selection as a running mate was "a big leap of faith" on the part of Senator McCain in an attempt to leave viewers with a negative impression regarding McCain's move. During the Headline News broadcast of the story, CNN underscored negative coverage regarding the issue with a caption that read, "Is she qualified to be a heartbeat away?" at the bottom of the screen. MSNBC followed suit by reporting on the story with the caption, "McCain made decision after "a single meeting and a phone call," at the bottom of the screen.

3 September 2008

A few days following Senator John McCain's announcement of then Governor Palin as his choice for Vice Presidential Republican Party nominee, a media firestorm erupted largely fueled by the news media's magnification of controversial stories involving Palin and her family. One issue involved her alleged involvement in the firing of at state official which was yet being investigated in her home state of Alaska. Another issue focused on the story broke by Senator John McCain's campaign that former Governor Palin's seventeen year old daughter, a senior in high school, was five months pregnant. Stories about the bombshell issue raised questions as to the former governor's fitness for duty as a Vice President in the wake of her daughter's teen pregnancy. Yet another story produced by the Media Political Machine's rumor mill had to do with the Governor's newborn, special needs child allegedly being her daughter's baby that Palin claimed as her own, as part of an elaborate cover up. For the most part, it was obvious that the media was stepping up its attack on the governor in efforts to discredit her as a serious Vice Presidential candidate much like its actions against Senator Clinton during her Presidential bid.

On the third day of the Republican National Convention, following Palin's address to the Republican assembly in Minneapolis, MSNBC's Keith Olbermann, hosting the network's evening commentary on the convention, helped to make the Media Political Machine's case against Palin. Almost immediately after Palin completed her speech for the acceptance of her party's nomination during the convention, Olbermann and guest panel members commented that Palin "gives a good speech," but insisted that her delivery on that evening "lacked substance." Correspondent Chris Matthews drew the conclusion that Palin was in no way comparable to Senator Hillary Clinton, and she instead presented a "cultural challenge" to Obama. Rookie, MSNBC Correspondent Rachel Maddow, who often displayed the grace of an SEC football coach when reporting, impressed upon viewers that Palin engaged in "mockery, sarcasm, and belittling," during her VP acceptance speech, which she directed at Senator Barack Obama. What was curious about this statement was that Maddow described the exact methods used by the Media Political Machine during broadcast after broadcast against Senator Clinton as she struggled to prove her relevance to the Democratic Party race for the presidential nomination. Correspondent David Gregory added that he felt as though Palin was being made into an "icon" prior to her nomination as the Vice President due to her lack of experience in many areas which was arguably the same campaign tactic being used by the news media in favor of Senator Barack Obama, however the news media seemed to have opportunely overlooked this. Additionally, Olbermann introduced a media manufactured poll that indicated Senator McCain's choice of then Governor Palin as a running mate for the '08 General Election made voters significantly less likely to support him for President.

TOXIC TACTICS:
Act As Though a Subject
Matter Expert

There are many different ways to become a subject matter expert in a given area. One could spend a great deal of time studying a certain field or performing functions on a repetitive basis in a particular capacity of employment. One could accumulate work experience in a given field for a prolonged period of time. One could also be responsible for a major breakthrough or facilitate the innovation in a given field to be regarded as a subject matter expert. One does *not*, however, become a subject matter expert simply by restating information, reading prepared information, or by hanging around those who have distinguished themselves in a particular field of study or area of concentration. Despite this, the news media has become notorious for knighting correspondents, reporters, and journalists subject matter experts on subjects ranging from politics to the economy, and from foreign affairs to health care merely because they have provided coverage in one or many of these areas at one time or another during the course of their careers. During the 2008 campaign season there was no end to the manner in which agents of the Media Political Machine worked themselves into roles of authority, providing what was passed off as "expert" commentary on almost every subject they provided coverage on. While most of our nation's leading correspondents that were so vocal and opinionative during the 2008 elections only held a journalism degree from an accredited institution at best, with the rare exception of those like MSNBC's Joe Scarborough and Rachel Maddow who hold more advanced degrees, that did not stop them from posing as economists, political advisors, or campaign analysts during the most critical periods of the 2008 campaign season.

The "Act as Though a Subject Matter Expert" toxic news reporting tactic was employed more frequently than any other tactic of a toxic nature by the American news media during the primaries and General Election of 2008. Instead of simply reporting facts in an objective manner and interviewing those who truly are subject matter experts regarding issues of national importance, news media correspondents and journalists repeatedly commented on every single story they presented as if they were trained experts in that particular field, giving viewers the false impression that they were listening to expert commentary which nine chances out of ten, could not have been farther from the truth. In most cases, the clear motive of the correspondent or journalist posing as an expert on a given subject during a broadcast or in a written work was to mislead readers, viewers, and voters alike to persuade them to agree with the position of the correspondent, journalist, or the media entity by which they were employed. One of the most appalling examples of this abuse of the public's trust using this highly toxic tactic took place during the height of the economic crisis of 2008 when the majority of American citizens were in a panic about the state of their investments and retirement funds that were vanishing before their eyes at lightning speed. CNN's Senior Business Correspondent Ali (pronounced Allie) Velshi, openly supported the proposed trillion dollar (Wall Street bailout) economic stimulus package proposed at the eleventh hour by the Bush Administration and sold like snake oil by the United States Congress, through singing its praises during several network broadcast segments. During the height of the debate period regarding the issue, Velshi used self interest driven rhetoric as well as economic jargon and fast talk to mislead viewers and voters with advice to support the stimulus package as a way to increase liquidity and free seized up credit within the market. Velshi even made a guest appearance on the "Oprah Winfrey Show," posing as a subject matter expert to explain the Wall Street bailout package to Winfrey's viewers. Velshi came under fire, however, shortly thereafter when several economic experts questioned his judgment regarding what should be done about the nation's economic woes during an evening network broadcast. The same experts also questioned Velshi's formal training and background in the field of economics from which he drew his positions and advised viewers. CNN's Website biography of Velshi revealed that though the network touted him as their "Senior Business Correspondent," and though he had covered many stories and hosted several shows devoted to business news, he only holds a degree in *Religion* from a Canadian university to show as formal education in any regard. Velshi's bio also revealed that he was at the time in the process of writing a book regarding financial management due out at the year's end.

To safeguard oneself against toxic reporting tactics of this nature, viewers and readers should rotate sources from which newsworthy information is gathered, thoroughly research the background of the person conveying the news story, and perform independent fact checks regarding information conveyed by agents of the news media as fact.

Some of the most opinionative individuals of the American news media during the 2008 campaign season have the following educational backgrounds:

Anderson Cooper, CNN Correspondent, Bachelors of Arts Degree in Political Science, Yale University

Gloria Borger, CNN Regular Guest Correspondent, Bachelor's Degree, Colgate University

John King, CNN Correspondent, Bachelors Degree in Journalism, University of Rhode Island

Campbell Brown, CNN Correspondent, Bachelors of Arts Degree in Political Science, Regis University

Suzanne Malveaux, CNN Correspondent, Bachelors Degree from Harvard University, Masters Degree in Journalism, Columbia University

Dana Bash, CNN Correspondent, Bachelors Degree, Political Communications, George Washington University

Candy Crowley, CNN Correspondent, Bachelors Degree, Randolph-Macon Women's College

Ali Velshi, CNN Senior Business Correspondent, Degree in Religion, Queens University (Canada)

Keith Olbermann, MSNBC Correspondent, Bachelors of Science Degree in Communications Arts, Cornell University

Rachel Maddow, MSNBC Correspondent, Doctorate Degree in Political Science, Oxford University (Rhodes Scholar)

Roland Martin, CNN Contributor, Bachelors Degree in Journalism, Texas A&M University

04 September 2008

As a dovetail to the initial smearing by the news media of the newest face of national politics, CBSNews.com featured a story titled "Alaska National Guard Hit "Crisis Level"[68] focused on the Alaska Air National Guard's struggle to fill its ranks, rendering it, according to CBS, "the most poorly staffed in the nation."[69] The story described the Alaska Air National Guard as having only 84% of its allocated positions filled, giving Alaska the lowest Air National Guard strength rating in the nation. What the story failed to point out is the fact that many National Guard units were experiencing the same issues regarding strength at the time due to multiple deployments and increased operational tempo associated with Operation Iraqi Freedom. The story also failed to note that due to Alaska's sparse population and its location in relation to the rest of the United States as well as difference in climate which negatively effects the ability to attract military personnel to the state, that there was not a lot that the Air National Guard could do about the situation at the time.

In addition to the disclosing of these half truths in the story, it went on to describe an internal situation in the Alaska Air National Guard in which the Alaska Adjutant General, appointed by Palin, made a policy that tied senior level officer promotions to recruiting and retention efforts to resolve the strength problem in the state Air National Guard ranks. Because Palin approved the state's two-star Adjutant General the award of a third star at the same time the Alaska Air Guard was experiencing strength woes, and due to the Adjutant General's policy regarding restricting promotions for senior level officers under his charge due to manning shortfalls, some "anonymous" Guardsmen complained of the act as hypocritical. Due to Palin's role as governor during Alaska National Guard's personnel strength "crisis," CBS News made a stretch of an attempt with this story to draw the conclusion that because of anemic personnel numbers in the state Air National Guard, Palin may not have been "qualified to be a heartbeat away from controlling the world's most powerful military." Sadly the correlation between Palin's service as the Governor of Alaska during a time when the state's National Guard was experiencing the very same troop strength issues as almost every other Guard force in the nation, and her qualifications to serve as the nation's Vice President was non-existent, making the network appear foolish for making such a poor attempt to smear Palin's public service record with such a thin justification.

On the same day, the CBS News Website also featured a story titled: "Sarah Palin Delivers Smash Hit In St. Paul."[70] The story, though listed under a heading for factual political news, was in all actuality an "analysis" which read more as a personal opinion hit-piece written by Vaughn Ververs who was listed as the network's senior political editor. Though at first glance, the very title of the story could easily lead one to believe the story was a favorable account of then Governor Palin's vice presidential nomination acceptance speech at the Republican National Convention, which was possibly by design to attract readers searching for more information on the Washington outsider, only a few lines into the story it was apparent this was definitely not the case. The first line of the story contained the phrase, "emerging from the shadows,"[71] as a reference to Palin's status as a political unknown, setting the tone for the negativity that was present throughout the piece. Though praise was given to Palin sparingly in the story, there was no shortage of negative innuendos and insinuations that rendered the story almost completely toxic in its obviously extremely biased form. Some of the statements that reeked of pessimism in reference to then Governor Palin included, "several rocky days in the national spotlight, her performance exceeded expectations, American's haven't exactly seen the most positive view of the new face, Palin's record has exposed some gaps between rhetoric and action," and," too many suspicions remain about her grasp of a range of issues."[72]

Though the story was terse, it was another veiled attack on a candidate during the 2008 campaign season. Despite its favorable title which insinuated the story was largely in reference to Palin's performance during her first campaign speech as Senator John McCain's choice for the Republican vice presidential nomination, the story instead took the low road of toxic news reporting that was more common than objectivity for the news media during the '08 campaign season. Any traces of intent for intellectual inclination or conveying factual information was entirely choked out by the weeds of bias and ill intent introduced by another agent of the

Media Political Machine. The closer viewers and voters alike got to the General Election, it was becoming increasingly harder to find news media outlets that provided information regarding any of the candidates left standing in the national presidential race that was not at least three parts bias, bull, or personal opinion.

07 September 2008

Limited media buzz ensued regarding rumors that indicated MSNBC hosts Keith Olbermann and Chris Matthews had been "demoted" at the network for grossly biased news reporting during the Republican National Convention in a disastrous move by the network to allow two of the most opinionative news commentators lead reporting roles during the convention. Though Olbermann and Matthews' toxic reporting antics had earned them a little time in the penalty box, it was arguable as to whether the move by the network to muzzle the two during the remainder of the election season was even a speed bump to the efforts of the Media Political Machine to control the outcome of the '08 elections through toxic news reporting since the disciplinary move was so subtle and not widely covered by the news media itself. There were dozens of news media correspondents that reflected equal or greater bias when reporting that were yet leading the charge against viewers and voters' right to make decisions regarding the elections based on the conveyance of factual information free of spin. Though it was doubtful that any in this group was oblivious to the actions taken by MSNBC against Olbermann and Matthews, it was also doubtful that such a minimal form of discipline, citing the retention by both of their respective shows, would have any effect on the toxic manner in which the appendages of the Media Political Machine would report news in the future.

10 September 2008

While many were still shocked at the maverick of Senator McCain's choice for a vice presidential running mate, and several news media entities were trying frantically to reverse the public's infatuation with then Governor Palin, Senator Obama found himself in the middle of a controversy regarding a statement he made at a campaign stop comparing the likeness of McCain's campaign platforms to that of President George W. Bush. Obama quipped that McCain's platform was simply the re-packaging of old ideas and like putting lipstick on a pig or wrapping an old fish in fresh paper. While Republicans over-dramatized the intent of the remark, screaming bloody murder over a remark that many of them, including Senator McCain, had made at various times during their political careers, many news media entities ran damage control for Senator Obama that was evident they would not have for any other candidate during the campaign season. A prime example of this was when the Media Political Machine pounced on Senator Hillary Clinton following a remark she made regarding the demographic makeup of her supporters during the primary elections. The news media did Clinton no favors in defusing the issue that took on a controversial nature when some insisted that Clinton was introducing race into the primary elections by making the remark. Instead, several news media correspondents supported the argument that Clinton was indeed playing the race card. Now, however, the Media Political Machine, instead of letting the Obama campaign deal with resolving the issue, was attempting to speak up for Senator Obama and insist that he was not referring to then Governor Palin as a pig with lipstick or Senator McCain as an old fish.

On the evening broadcast of "Hardball with Chris Matthews," Matthews made a very compelling argument that Republicans were making too much of an issue of the lipstick and old fish controversy. He challenged a Republican strategist on the show by asking her how she knew that Senator Obama was making a jab at Senator McCain and former Governor Palin through his use of a very commonly used saying. It was however unfortunate that media correspondents, such as Matthews, did not feel as compelled to come to the defense of other candidates when they experienced controversy as the result of words uttered as they did for Senator Obama. CBSNews.com also provided its version of damage control with a story posted on the network's site titled "Obama Under Fire For Lipstick Remark."[73] While the story started out as objective in regards to the issue, about halfway through the story, a quote from CBSNews.com senior political editor Vaughn Ververs provided advice from the news media to the

Obama campaign which was a common occurrence. Ververs wrote: "This is just the kind of discussion that the Obama campaign does not want to be caught up in right now, whether it's a manufactured controversy or not." Again, the providing of political advice, was a common courtesy afforded the Obama campaign by the Media Political Machine, unsolicited, yet not afforded other candidates when they experienced challenges during their campaigns. This well documented occurrence made it all too obvious that the news media had a clear favorite during the campaign and would stop at nothing to facilitate his rise to the Oval Office.

TOXIC TACTICS:
Sweep It Under the Rug
(AKA Damage Control)

As election season 2008 was one of the most important and divisive ever in the history of our democracy, news media efforts to determine the ultimate outcome of the primaries and General Election were easily identifiable in almost every broadcast and story produced. Though many tactics of ill intent were used by the news media to persuade viewers and voters to feel this way or that regarding a candidate or given issue, one of the most easily identifiable tactics employed by leading network correspondents and political journalists during the 2008 elections was the old "Sweep It Under the Rug" method of dealing with stories it wished eliminated from the front lines of media coverage.

Using this toxic tactic, hardly detectable when occurring though blazingly obvious upon reflection, the Media Political Machine rendered itself the ultimate decider regarding "the issues important to the people" versus those that were not through providing minimal coverage of issues detrimental to its agenda. For example, at the height of the controversy surrounding Senator Barack Obama and longtime pastor Reverend Jeremiah Wright, correspondents and journalists of almost all major news media outlets actively participated in damage control efforts to make the story seem of little importance to viewers and voters, and make Senator Obama seem completely in the dark regarding controversial statements Wright made while delivering various documented sermons, therefore attempting to sweep the issue under the rug. Though Obama attended the church Wright pastored, for over twenty years, was married to wife Michelle by Wright, and referred to Wright, at one point during his campaign as "like an uncle" to him, media pundits insisted Obama was never a witness to Wright's sometimes racially charged and often controversial sermons despite twenty years of regular attendance at the church of which the Obamas were members. One media correspondent even went as far as to characterize Senator Obama as "genuinely hurt" by controversial statements Wright made while attending at least two events during Obama's presidential campaign, one being a widely televised NAACP National Convention. Beyond this, the news media diverted attention from the issue by demonizing another popular candidate involved in the Democratic Party nomination process, at the time, for issues of far less importance than the one that dogged Senator Obama. The news media then quickly and steadily decreased coverage regarding Obama's possible approval of the religious, social, and political ideas that Wright spoke about so passionately, as efficiently as it turned off coverage of the war raging in Iraq and Afghanistan, and the mounting casualties that resulted during the time of the elections. Similar action was taken by the news media when Senator Obama made a controversial statement regarding Pennsylvanians being "bitter" and clinging to "guns and religion" as a result of experiencing an increasingly difficult economic situation. In sharp contrast to the news media's efforts to sweep select issues under the rug in regards to then Senator Obama, when Alaskan former Governor Palin's controversial "Troopergate" story broke into national headlines, the news media made no attempt to progressively move the story away from the forefront of political news coverage or to find some other political candidate to demonize during the height of the controversy.

Viewers and readers of news media generated stories should beware of the "Sweep It Under the Rug" toxic news reporting tactic as it was employed aggressively by the Media Political Machine during election season 2008 in a manner that promoted easily noticeable bias into coverage that should have remained entirely objective, allowing for voters to make informed decisions unfettered. It is often said in southern society, "when people start talking to you about the weather, keep your hand on your wallet," because it is possible that someone wants to divert your attention from the real issue at hand by raising issues of little or no importance to you at the same time. The same was true of the American news media's efforts to sweep several issues of national importance and concern under the rug during the '08 elections in an attempt to steer the will of American voters by providing only limited coverage regarding certain controversial issues, while hypocritically providing maximum coverage regarding negative issues embattling those not in its favor.

11 September 2008

As November fast approached, the General Election contest between Senator Barack Obama and Senator John McCain intensified in the area of campaign rhetoric through the airing of a commercial paid for by the McCain for President Campaign regarding a sex education bill allegedly supported by Obama while he was a yet an Illinois state legislator. The commercial was obviously an attempt by the McCain campaign to bring into question Senator Obama's judgment regarding the controversial issue of sex education and when it was appropriate for school aged children to be exposed to it. Though the commercial used both strong and accusatory language that could easily be regarded as political smearing, MSNBC.com took up the cross for Senator Obama, running interference and damage control through posting a story to the network run site written by Larry Rohter of *The New York Times*, admonishing the McCain campaign for distorting key facts regarding the issue. Though the story did not originate at MSNBC, the network made it a point to post the story, arguing on Senator Obama's behalf, much like Media Political Machine's efforts, only a day prior, to facilitate damage control operations regarding the "lipstick on a pig" flap. Again, this was a courtesy extended to Senator Obama, unsolicited, that was not afforded to any other candidate by the news media who often dog piled other candidates experiencing difficulties due to controversies during the course of their campaigns. This was also not a responsibility of the news media who would better serve program viewers and Website surfers by presenting facts regarding this and other controversial issues and leaving rebuttals and damage control efforts to the offended campaign who had more than adequate campaign coffers to do so.

In a story titled: "Sex-ed ad distorts Obama policy,"[74] Rohter argued convincingly that the McCain campaign ad was grossly misleading then defended Obama as a strong supporter of education reform as he alleged the McCain campaign commercial reduced Obama's record on education to supporting sex education for children even before they learned to read. Rohter also included quotes from Obama clarifying his stance on the touchy subject. The publishing of this article by an arm of the news media was perfectly alright as an opinion or editorial piece, however by its being posted to MSNBCs Website as political news, though written by an author not employed by the network, it was glaringly obvious that the network was doing its best to part from the road of objectivity and favor Senator Obama's candidacy since it almost never defended other candidates during the 2008 election season. With Rohter's words, "the McCain campaign is largely recycling old and discredited accusations made against Mr. Obama by Alan Keyes in their 2004 Senate race,"[75] the bias exhibited by the news media was again reaffirmed due to agents of the Media Political Machine writing and posting the rebuke of the McCain campaign ad rather than allowing for a response from the Obama campaign, and reporting the facts of its content.

12 September 2008

As a dovetail to the unsolicited damage control efforts made by the news media on behalf of Senator Obama the day before, regarding the sex education for kindergarteners controversy initiated by an arguably below the belt McCain campaign ad, MSNBC.com posted a story smearing Cindy McCain under its "US, World, Politics" section. While, again, the story was not an original, but instead lifted from the pages of *The Washington Post*, it seemed to be another in a long list of efforts by the Media Political Machine to go on the attack in pursuit of some of those involved in the 2008 presidential election process. This time it was a scathing attack on the character and integrity of a potential future First Lady. "Cindy McCain's tangled addiction story, consequences of her drug abuse were more complex than she's portrayed,"[76] was a story written by Kimberly Kindy of *The Washington Post* and stealthily listed on MSNBC News' Website under the stories, "Obama shifts to attack mode as party frets," and "Palin fuzzy on foreign policy." It was a story that broke originally during Senator McCain's 2000 election campaign and was being raised from the dead by the news media grasping for anything to counter the slight momentum gained by the 2008 McCain campaign following the Senator's controversial selection of then Governor Sarah Palin as a vice presidential running mate. While the story was written in the form of an editorial, MSNBC listed the story on its Website right alongside the latest news, most of which was free from spin, and presented factual information free of unsolicited opinion. This manner of listing the story gave the false impression that all commentary in the story by Kindy was, though obviously well researched, presented in an entirely factual and objective manner.

The main purpose of Kindy's story was easily understood as one which critically shed more light on the resurrected Cindy McCain drug addiction story while simultaneously casting doubt on the integrity of both Cindy and John McCain as when Kindy wrote in regards to a seemingly lenient prosecution of Cindy during her legal battles related to the addiction while also mentioning Senator McCain drew the "mildest sanction"[77] of anyone prosecuted as a result of the Keating Five scandal. Throughout the story it was clear that though Cindy McCain had repeatedly addressed the issue of past drug abuse struggles, Kindy was not so convinced that she was being completely honest about the situation. Kindy wrote about Cindy McCain's explanation in regards to resolving her issue with drug addiction: "She has not discussed what kind of treatment she received for her addiction, but she has made clear that she *believes* she has put her problems behind her,"[78] as if to say that McCain is only a pill away from going down the same path of drug abuse in the future. Kindy also wrote in the opening paragraphs of the story: "While McCain's accounts have captured the pain of her addiction, her journey through this personal crisis is a more complicated story than she has described, and it had more consequences for her and those around her than she has acknowledged."[79] The remainder of Kindy's story included seemingly factual accounts surrounding the legal ramifications of McCain's drug addiction as it related to the non-profit medical service organization through which she obtained some of the drugs she was addicted to. The story, at the same time, reflected the author's effort to dig for more dirt surrounding the events of the issue to make the story seem worse in nature than had been revealed by media outlets previously.

While *The Washington Post* story regarding Cindy McCain's drug addiction issues was highly opinionative, and in many regards toxic, due to timing of its release. The story further took on a heightened toxic nature by being posted to the MSNBC News Website that day, because it gave the impression, through being listed with stories based on current and almost completely factual information, that it was also mostly factual in nature instead of largely the opinion of the author supported by circumspectly selected facts. As the story was listed on MSNBC.com, it took on the nature of a smear tactic against both McCains due to its being listed under the political news section at a time in which the McCain campaign was doing relatively well against the Obama campaign seeking to regain its footing following the announcement that Palin was John McCain's choice to be the Vice President. In addition to this, MSNBC made no effort to list a story, for the sake of objectivity, digging into the ashes of Senator Obama's admission to experiencing limited drug abuse when he was much younger. After all, he was a contender for the highest office in our nation's government while Cindy McCain was not. Instead of affording equitable treatment to those involved in the election process of 2008, which sometimes included candidates' family members, the news media continued to pick and choose who it smeared and involved in the Media Political Campaign's efforts to influence viewers and voters using toxic conveyance of information for its own political gain—power over the electorate.

19 September 2008

The closer the nation came to the 2008 General Election, the more toxic the reporting from the Media Political Machine became as evidenced by MSNBC's allowing for entire programs to be devoted to extreme biased news reporting. These programs offered very little in the way of reporting factual information and were instead marked by exaggerated antics for purposes of entertaining, and by the conveying of highly opinionative information which hosting correspondents passed off as fact. One of the worst offenders of this form of toxic news reporting was the recently reprimanded and recently demoted co-host of MSNBC's "Race for the White House," former sports news correspondent, Keith Olbermann, host of MSNBC's "Countdown with Keith Olbermann."

On this evening's broadcast of his show, Olbermann lit into the McCain-Palin campaign like a laser guided missile, initially criticizing Senator McCain for making several missteps of the spoken word during the week while on the campaign trail, referring to the names of various governmental agencies in an erroneous manner, which the news media often pointed out during the campaign season as a sign that an aging McCain was not as sharp minded as he once was. Olbermann went on to dedicate his *entire* show to the bashing of Senator McCain and former Governor Palin in a manner that proved balance and fairness in news reporting was now virtually non-existent and seemingly condoned by the networks that supported its abolishment through filling prime broadcast time slots with programs of this nature. Olbermann made the country's deteriorating economic situation the launch pad for his program, insisting the government's $85 million bailout of insurance giant AIG, and the announced bankruptcy of other pillars of the American economy spelled out a bad week for Senator McCain and Republicans. Throughout the program Olbermann used clips of Obama speaking on the campaign trail during the week as well as official Obama campaign statements as skillfully as one of Senator Obama's own presidential campaign staffers, as if he was, like many other news media correspondents seemed to be, campaigning for the position of White House Press Secretary in the event of an Obama victory.

Guests on Olbermann's evening broadcast included Obama supporter and author of "Obamanomics" a book regarding how the "bottom up" Obama plan of economics was the answer to American economic woes, John Talbott. During Olbermann's interview of Talbott, at least five clips of past footage containing Senator McCain standing or walking alongside President George Bush were played in efforts to send the subliminal message that Bush and McCain were one and the same as often stated by the Obama presidential campaign. Olbermann also interviewed Christopher Hayes of *The Nation* who pointed out Senator McCain once supported President Bush's plan of investing social security monies into the stock market which was a very unpopular idea with the American public. This argument by a guest of Olbermann's show served as reinforcement to the idea of McCain and Bush's ideology being fundamentally identical regarding most political issues.

Olbermann switched gears on the broadcast from highlighting likenesses between Senator McCain and embattled lame duck

President George W. Bush only to devote the second half of his program to a tabloid styled news reporting attack on McCain's vice presidential running mate, former Governor Sarah Palin. Olbermann introduced a story straight from the back pages of the *National Enquirer* that focused on a minister who Olbermann characterized as a modern day witch hunter who also allegedly was given credit by former Governor Palin for her successful campaign for the governorship of Alaska. The latter was never proven during the broadcast though footage was played in which Palin described how Pastor Thomas Moothy of the World Faith Church in Alaska prayed for God to "make a way" for her to perform the duties of the office of governor. Despite this, Olbermann insisted that Palin gave significant credit for her campaign victory to Pastor Moothy who made Reverend Jeremiah Wright, as Olbermann described him, "seem like Father Flannigan from Boys Town."[80] Olbermann also cited a report by the *Times of London* that Moothy was responsible for the expulsion of a woman from a town in Kenya due to his labeling her a "witch" and declaring she was to blame for several automobile accidents in the town.[81] The sole purpose of the story highlighting Palin's relationship with Moothy seemed to be to draw a correlation between the controversy that once dogged Obama regarding his longtime pastor Reverand Wright, and Palin's relationship with Reverend Moothy who was never identified as her pastor.

Olbermann concluded his campaign smearing broadcast with his latest gimmick, which was almost as silly and pointless as his "World's Worst" person of the day. On this night, he pledged to give $100 to charity every time then Governor Palin told what he deemed to be a lie during the remainder of the presidential campaign, which he stated was a common occurrence that she never took responsibility for.[82] Lies Olbermann concluded Palin told during the week included statements she made regarding the now famous Bridge to Nowhere, her statement regarding taking a voluntary pay cut as the governor of Alaska, statements regarding "Troopergate," and those she made regarding posting the Alaska Governor's plane for sale on ebay. By Olbermann's count which included $100 to charity every time the statements were made during the week even if it was multiple times about the same issue, Palin lied 37 times prompting him to mockingly write a $3700 check to the Alaska Special Olympics during the broadcast and sealing it in a pre-addressed stamped envelope, all during his live broadcast.

This form of ultra-biased toxic news reporting was, again, becoming more and more common and extreme from multiple news media outlets the closer the nation came to the November elections, with some media news networks even adding programs to the daily broadcast lineup to reinforce the news media offensive through repetition of toxic attacks on certain candidates while serving as a pep squad for others. This was made most noticeable with the addition of the "Rachel Maddow Show" on MSNBC which was supplementary to the network's nightly biased news lineup following shows featuring Chris Matthews and Keith Olbermann, both of which were said to have been recently reprimanded by the network for extreme bias as co-hosts of MSNBC's "Race For the White House" now hosted by correspondent David Gregory. The sometimes unpolished Maddow, who would be arguably better suited for commentating on a sports news show, was to some degree even less objective in her delivery than Matthews or Olbermann while covering regurgitated toxic news from both their preceding shows each evening.

On the evening of 18 September 2008, Maddow opened her show by making fun of Senator John McCain's verbal slip up during an interview regarding a possible meeting with President Zapatero of Spain, in the event of McCain's election to the presidency. During the interview, McCain mistook Zapatero for the leader of a South American nation, obviously due to his unfamiliarity with the name of Spain's current leader. Maddow, however made a major issue of the interview in a manner that made it seem as if the misstep was much more important than it actually was, reflecting negatively on Senator McCain's knowledge regarding the identity of world leaders during the presidential campaign. Maddow's exaggerated antics regarding McCain's latest campaign gaffe bordered on the same "mockery, sarcasm, and belittling" she pointed out as a shortcoming of former Governor Palin's address to the Republican National Convention on September 3rd as Palin spewed partisan rhetoric directed at Democrats. Following Maddow's opening assault on Senator McCain, she interviewed Senator Jim Webb regarding comments made by Senator Chuck Hagel who cited Palin's lack of foreign relations experience. Webb commented that support of then Governor Palin as a viable vice presidential nominee would require a "great leap of faith" by the American people. Next, Maddow interviewed longtime Clinton campaign strategist and advisor Paul Begala. Maddow used the interviews of Webb and Begala as a springboard to direct more partisan rhetoric of her own at Senator McCain during the broadcast. After briefly visiting a few of the show's entertainment gimmicks to round out the relentlessly biased and unbalanced show, Maddow talked unconvincingly about why the McCain Palin campaign ticket failed to draw the support of disgruntled Hillary Clinton supporters. She then ended the show by snidely commenting on how the Alaska "Troopergate" investigation had successfully been "quashed" by former Governor Palin until after the General Election and cited Palin's husband and aide's refusal to cooperate with the investigation. What Maddow opportunely failed to cover during her show, however, was how the Media Political Machine that employed her and did her script writing quashed countless news stories and issues of controversy involving candidates favored by the news media during the 2008 elections while manipulating the type and amount of coverage it provided others that found themselves outside of its favor.

22 September 2008

Jonathan Mahler, a contributing writer for the *New York Times Magazine* published an article in *Newsweek* magazine dated 29 September, 2008 titled "The Ur-Text of a Tabloid Age."[83] The article was a very well written and stirring analysis of tabloid type news reporting that made several digs at the *National Enquirer*, which was arguably the king of news reporting focused on scandal and issues of a controversial nature often shunned by the mainstream news media. In one section of the lengthy, in depth article, Mahler made the declaration that America's major news organizations still saw themselves as "public servants" regarding the craft of reporting information in its purest and most factual form, supported by credible sources. Mahler added the fast fact that the Federal Trade Commission once "mandated" that major news networks set up respective news divisions to "keep the citizenry well informed,"[84] which he argued was not a hallmark of tabloid news reporting.

What Mahler failed to point out, however, in his firm defense of the mainstream media, that he characterized as so dedicated to serving American society through reporting carefully researched truths, was the fact that the news media had long since gone on sabbatical leave from its *mandated* duties to pursue a more entertaining and opinionative form of news reporting that rivaled the methods of reporting employed by tabloids.

Never was a case of dereliction of duty so evident as during election season '08 when the mainstream news media took the low road of news reporting through both overtly and covertly orchestrating a political campaign of its own in efforts to control the outcome both the nation's primary and General Elections for the presidency. For over eighteen straight months, the Media Political Machine engaged in toxic news reporting that was based more on the opinion of the conveyor, in this case reporters and journalists, than it was based on cold hard facts. Much like the tabloids, the American news media employed reporting tactics during the election season that signified it was more concerned with the need to receive good ratings and move copies than with conveying information in an objective manner as in the case of the nation's leading magazines that featured Senator Barack Obama on over twenty eight covers during the campaign season, including *Newsweek* magazine which featured Senator Obama on six of its covers during the elections. *Time* magazine also featured the same lack of objectivity by featuring Senator Obama on eight magazine covers during the elections while scarcely giving any top shelf newsstand visual publicity to other candidates involved in the 2008 election process for party nominations and the presidency. While news media magazines engaged in overtly biased conveyance of information it deemed newsworthy, leading television news networks engaged in biased reporting as well as smear campaigns against those most competitive to their unanimous choice for the presidency. This was evidenced most conspicuously in the case of Senator Hillary Clinton and husband, former President Bill Clinton, who were relentlessly attacked by correspondents of MSNBC, CNN, and at times CBS news networks during Hillary's campaign for the Democratic Party nomination. The same was true when Senator Clinton was eliminated from the campaign race and former Governor Sarah Palin gave the campaign of Senator John McCain a much needed boost of momentum. When it seemed as though the McCain campaign was moving ahead in the opinion polls, the news media networks let the dogs loose on both Palin and McCain in the same negative manner that it did when it facilitated the destruction of the Clinton campaign for the Democratic Party nomination in 2008. As a testament to this, a Pew Research Center, Journalism.org author wrote the following regarding MSNBC's biased coverage, at the time, in a story titled, "Cable—Three Different Networks, Three Different Perspectives:"[85] "At that point McCain was enjoying a post-convention bounce that had vaulted him into the lead in most national polls. The media generally were also focused on Palin's ability to energize the Republican base. But that week on MSNBC, McCain and Palin's narratives were more negative than positive (for Palin overwhelmingly so) while Obama got more positive coverage overall."[86]

Another notable point made by Jonathan Mahler in defense of the mainstream news media's methods of reporting, which he cited as more noble than that of tabloids, was that reporters assigned to cover the Monica Lewinsky scandal in 1998 exercised some form of restraint that other none mainstream news outlets chose to bypass. Mahler stated, "if anything, the whole sorry saga left the media even more conflicted about whether to root around in the private lives of politicians, particularly when there were no clear public consequences at stake."[87] As I remembered it personally, however, any restraint the news media exercised during the Clinton years regarding the Monica Lewinsky scandal was imperceptible, because almost every correspondent and reporter associated with it, in concert with the Republican Party, made it a point to dig as far into the matter as humanly possible. The same restraint exercising mainstream news media that Jonathan Mahler spoke so fondly of, also dragged the remnants of the scandal onto the political stage in 2008, haunting the campaign of Senator Clinton, during the Democratic primary elections and leading up to Senator Obama's unveiling of his choice for a vice presidential running mate going into the General Election. A full ten years later, the news media exercised no restraint when referring to the "baggage" that the Clintons carried as a low key insinuation that there were still traces of infidelity and scandal hovering over them that voters should take issue with.

Jonathan Mahler's *Newsweek* article was typical of mainstream news media agents that find it fairly easy to point out the faults of other media outlets while turning a blind eye to the frequent transgressions of the American news media. In 2008 there was no shortage of tabloid styled news reporting from the *National Enquirer* or the mainstream Media Political Machine. The difference, however, was the fact that American society expected this form of news reporting from the *National Enquirer* but not from the news media that, as Mahler pointed out, was once charged by the Federal Communications Commission with keeping the citizens of this nation well informed but unfortunately employed toxic news reporting tactics during the '08 election season in doing so.

23 September 2008

A story titled, "NRA Begins Push to Tarnish Obama On Guns,"[88] written by CBSNews.com political reporter Brian Montopoli was posted to the CBS News Website in efforts to inform readers of a campaign being launched by the National Rifle Association against Senator Barack Obama in an attempt to smear him as being an "anti-gun" presidential candidate. The story opened by vividly describing an ad that ran in three states by the NRA featuring a middle aged white Virginian man dressed in hunting gear. At one point in the ad, the man turned to the camera and made a pointed accusation regarding Senator Obama wanting to put "a huge tax" on his guns and ammo. The old man then stated "he's probably never been hunting a day in his life."[89] Montopoli cited a statement the *Washington Post* issued, saying the NRA ad was a "huge stretch" based on a nine year old vaguely-worded newspaper article. From that point, Montopoli put on his Obama campaign staffer hat and, just as had become common practice among the news media ranks, proceeded to defend Obama, slamming the ad using quotes from Obama's vice presidential running mate and others to push his obviously pro-Obama agenda.

While the story was very well written and thoroughly researched, it was chock full of the same hypocrisy that ran rampant through the ranks of the Media Political Machine, pointing out the politically motivated transgressions of other entities while wallowing in its own.

The story yet again reinforced the brazen two-facedness of the news media during the '08 elections when Montopoli boldly pointed out that the "NRA's political arm" had launched a campaign to smear Obama, using four new television ads on cable networks in three states in addition to similar ads on radio and in print.[90] Montopoli did not, however, inform readers that the NRA's measly three state campaign during the remainder of the dwindling campaign season paled in comparison to the nation-wide campaign run by the political arm of the American news media during the entire eighteen months of the campaign season in which it attacked political candidates and their campaigns, with increasing intensity, using multiple news networks, magazines, newspapers and other such outlets in a concerted effort that proved disastrous to the campaign efforts of numerous victims. It seemed that Montopoli as well as his news media colleagues had completely overlooked or conveniently forgotten about the misleading words of ill intent and deceit that so many of the Media Political Machine's agents spewed during the 2008 elections seeking to control the outcome of the democratic election process for purposes of both increased political power and financial gain.

26 September 2008

With five weeks left to go before one of the most important General Elections in American history as well as that of the world, the American news media had returned to operating on full throttle with regard to reporting tactics lacking in objectivity. Correspondent David Gregory, now the host of MSNBC's "Race for the White House," show dedicated to up to the minute coverage of the 2008 presidential election, tried his hardest to appear objective in his news reporting during each broadcast, especially following the ouster of Keith Olbermann and Chris Matthews from the reporting desk due to flagrantly overt bias in delivery. This particular evening he interviewed several members of Congress regarding the 700 billion dollar bailout proposal made by President Bush and Chief of the Securities and Exchange Commission to bolster the downward spiral of the American economy due to poor oversight by the government and poor business decisions made by the nation's largest savings and loans institutions. While Gregory asked the congressmen interviewed some very pointed but fair questions, grilling them about the involvement of both Obama and McCain in the process of passing the multi-billion dollar bailout package that was at the time ill received by American society, he also took a brief detour from objective news reporting to revisit a subject often brought up by agents of the news media during the period following Senator Obama's official nomination as the Democratic Party's presidential candidate. Quite clever in his delivery, Gregory injected his brand of toxicity as the show's new lead correspondent through using leading, partisan questions, leaving it to those he interviewed to take the reins on delivering partisan rhetoric motivated largely by the questions he chose to ask. This often successfully left Gregory seeming completely fair and balanced in his presentation. Upon closer inspection, however, for the discriminating viewer, it was easy to detect the toxicity and hidden agenda of his news reporting tactics. Though arguably more objective than other correspondents employed by MSNBC, Gregory was biased in his delivery nonetheless, albeit more refined.

On the evening broadcast of "Race for the White House," Gregory displayed his true colors as prominently as the network's mascot while interviewing guest, former U.S. Congressman Harold Ford Jr. of Tennessee. Gregory again introduced "The Clinton Factor," as had become a common practice of numerous news media networks and publications seeking to exploit the campaign skills of Senator and former President Clinton to aid Senator Obama in his bid for control of the Oval Office. Gregory, true to Media Political Machine agent form, made the comment to Ford that *some people* did not feel that the former President and Senator were doing enough to support Senator Obama's campaign for the presidency. Former Congressman Ford skillfully dodged the media land mine set for him by Gregory, insisting that former President and Senator Clinton were actively engaged in supporting Obama's campaign and would do more to support him in the coming days as it grew closer to the General Election. Though Gregory quipped he was "not feeling the love," in reference to the Clintons' support for the Obama campaign, there was now, curiously, no mention of the "baggage" that the news media so adamantly insisted the Clintons carried with them during Senator Clinton's campaign for the Democratic Party nomination.

While there was no end to declaration of the existence of this "baggage" during Clinton's bid for her party's nomination, it was now apparent that the news media had done a complete, hypocritical about face by insisting that the Clintons were now the key to Senator Obama's success in the upcoming campaign days. With the raising of this issue, marking such a clearly defined contrast in the rhetoric of the news media in regards to the Clintons during the 2008 elections, Gregory positively identified himself as a card carrying member of the same Media Political Machine that so brazenly injected toxicity and self interest into the coverage of the primaries and the General Election.

28 September 2008

The first presidential debate of the seemingly never ending campaign season, featured Senator John McCain, the Republican Party nominee, and Senator Barack Obama, the Democratic Party nominee, in a head to head political match up. The debate took place at Ole Miss University in Oxford, Mississippi on the evening of 26 September. Following the widely viewed and often spirited debate between two of the most prominent figures in the history of American politics, the race was on in the cut rooms of the mainstream news media to convince American viewers and voters who actually emerged as the victor of the first presidential debate of such a hotly contested campaign season. While spin masters of the Media Political Machine presented standard unverifiable independent polls and interviewed biased broadcast regulars it yet referred to as "guests," and while leading media correspondents made arguments for who won the debate as convincingly as strategists actually employed by the respective campaigns, the *Arkansas Democrat Gazette* newspaper published a story titled "1st debate: Both claim they won,"[91] in its Sunday edition that reflected balance and objectivity other mainstream news media outlets found it so hard to produce.

In the introductory paragraphs of the story contributed to by several Associated Press and *The New York Times* writers, verifiable facts were presented regarding the percentage of the nation's population that tuned in to the debates from a source outside the newspaper rather than by simply making up polling data to support an agenda of ill intent and persuade readers to think one way or the other. This, at the time, was a practice that was almost none existent in regards other news media outlets that most often chose to manufacture their own data and provide little if any reference to its origin. The story then succeeded in objectively covering what each of the campaigns was doing to maximize their efforts to spin the debate in favor of their candidate, first covering one campaign then the other, being careful not to give the perception of bias in favor of one candidate over the other. "The positioning was in keeping what is now a quadrennial rite in which the campaigns go full-bore to convince the news media, and ultimately the public, that their candidate won,"[92] wrote the story's author referring to campaign efforts to spin the debate outcome in favor of one candidate or the other. This common practice and its natural order was somehow reversed by news media entities such as CNN that saw fit to initiate its own spin campaign, originating from broadcast regulars and host correspondents, superseding any efforts of the respective political campaigns to perform the duties for which they were paid, and declaring victory for its own respective candidate. The toxic efforts many mainstream news media outlets used to report the outcome of the debate, however, reflected the same favor for their chosen victor witnessed by avid followers of national politics for the preceding eighteen months. Absent from Media Political Machine reports regarding the debate was, as always, any verifiable data that could even remotely support the arguments put forth by its loyal agents.

Arkansas' leading and most widely circulated newspaper, in its story regarding the debate, also elaborated on the activities of each candidate the day following the debate, citing reliable campaign sources that informed the author that Senator McCain returned to campaign headquarters in Washington to make key phone calls to congressional leaders while Senators Obama and Biden made a campaign stop in Greensboro, North Carolina that drew a line of supporters stretching eight to ten blocks. The story further reported the campaign efforts of Michelle Obama and Jill Biden, as well as that of Senator Hillary Clinton who was on the stump for Obama in Michigan. The Dem Gaz rounded out the informative and balanced story by outlining the goals of each candidate going into the first debate, writing in regards to Obama, "it was to show that he had the stature to serve as commander in chief, and present himself as the proper steward for the turbulent economy."[93] About McCain's goal the author wrote, "it was to move past a topsy-turvy week for the economy and his campaign, and establish his pre-eminence on national security while raising doubts about Obama."[94] Nowhere in the story was it evident as to what the personal opinion of the author was, or his personal preference for who should serve as the country's next president as was almost always center stage on broadcasts of leading news media outlets and in the most popular news media publications during campaign season '08. The author did not express contempt for either candidate, preference for one over the other, nor did he attempt to lead readers in a pre-determined direction of thinking. The story was written in a manner that made it evident that serious and devoted agents of the news media still existed with the ability to deliver newsworthy factual information to viewers allowing for them to make their own determination as to who was the best candidate for them. What was more was the fact that a newspaper with the name *Arkansas Democrat Gazette* was capable of producing such an unbiased story during a campaign season so inundated with partisan rhetoric. The story was a testament to the professionalism of the newspaper and its staff's dedication to delivering readers facts instead of opinions regarding such an important presidential debate, at a time when the future of the nation's continued existence as a respected world leader hung in the balance. While there were plenty of opinions available for those who cared to read them regarding issues ranging from that of local, to national, to international concern, as was the case with most serious newspapers at the time, the Dem Gaz left that form of reporting to the editorial section complete with the heading "EDITORIALS" as a distinguishing disclaimer.

CNN correspondent Fareed Zakaria, host of "Fareed Zakaria GPS," conducted an interview of Premier Wen Jiabao of China which also aired on this day.[95] During the introduction to the weekly broadcast, Zakaria spoke about the conditions of the interview due to the fact that the Chinese seldom allowed interviews by the Western media. The condition requested to be agreed upon by CNN and Zakaria was that Zakaria could ask Premier Jiabao any question that he wanted to. The condition requested by the Chinese government and Premier Jiabao was that Zakaria would not comment on or characterize the interview either during or following its taping. Both sides agreed to the other's condition and the interview took place as scheduled.

I found it very interesting that the Chinese government knew enough about the American news media to know that biased commentary and characterization was a commonality, and that it could quickly change the point of the interview and the meaning of any answer Premier Jiabao gave to Zakaria's questions. I further found it sad that the world seemed aware of the toxicity of the nation's news media yet many of our nation's citizens, that spent years and years listening to the likes of Walter Cronkite, Dan Rather, and Bernard Shaw were yet unaware that the news media had morphed into an entity with a hidden agenda that could seldom be trusted as alluded to by the Chinese government's condition for Premier Jiabao's interview with CNN's Zakaria. It then became apparent to me exactly why many foreign nations are very guarded as to how they choose to deal with the American news media, if they choose to do so at all. It was also made clear to me, through the Chinese government's interview precondition, that Senator John McCain's campaign refused to allow campaign embeds from the Media Political Machine into its camp during the '08 election season because it could do the campaign more harm than good. This fact was most evident during the 2008 elections when news media correspondents embedded with the Clinton campaign chose to report negative issues with the inner workings of the campaign, often times referring to it as "disorganized," instead of providing unbiased updates regarding the latest campaign stop and what took place that day along the campaign trail. Future campaigns would do good to agree upon media embed coverage with preconditions as in the case of the Chinese government to prevent toxic news reporting from destroying it from within as was a tactic used by the Media Political Machine most effectively against the Clinton campaign for the Democratic Party nomination in 2008.

1 October 2008

With the mounting woes of a failing economy, the collapse of multiple financial institutions vital to the stability of the American economy, and a Congress deadlocked on whether to support a $700 billion Wall Street bail out package at the expense of American tax payers, the most prominent institutions of the American news media continued a campaign to exercise its toxic influence on the populace through the disproportionate use of biased rhetoric. Though the Media Political Machine held fast, unwaveringly, to many of its campaign positions during the 2008 election season, it was also becoming more prone to flip flops as in the case of the presidential candidates themselves during the balance of the campaign season. The latest flip flop on the part of the news media came, of course, from the "most trusted" of the nation's news networks when on 1 October, John Roberts, while hosting CNN's Election Center evening broadcast, asked a panel of three regulars about their views regarding former President Clinton's campaign efforts in support of Senator Barack Obama. At the time the former President had recently made a campaign stop for Obama in Florida that drew a sizeable crowd of Obama supporters. Among the panel members was CNN Senior Political Analyst Gloria Borger who was among one of the most outspoken agents of the news media to verbalize her disapproval of both Senator and former President Clinton during Senator Clinton's campaign for the Democratic Party nomination for the presidency.

Earlier in the 2008 election season, Correspondent Gloria Borger was a frequent participant in network panels that closely scrutinized the political process surrounding the elections. She was an active participant on several CNN panels in which she held the position that former President Clinton was wrong when he made the assumption that the news media was possibly the facilitator of an "anti-Clinton campaign" during the '08 elections, Senator Clinton could not empower the Barack Obama for President Campaign by being selected as his vice presidential running mate, and the widely held sentiment among agents of the news media that Senator Clinton should suspend her campaign and concede to Senator Obama even before the primary election process was completed. Though Borger often spoke quite unflatteringly of both Clintons during Senator Clinton's campaign, on 1 October, she joined a panel hosted by correspondent John Roberts that unanimously agreed that the former President was the best thing since sliced bread in regards to his campaign efforts that had been redirected to support Senator Obama for the presidency. Not one of the panel members assembled on this evening had anything negative to say about the former President who met with unbridled scrutiny and criticism from the Media Political Machine and the agents it employed during the presidential campaign of Senator Clinton. Most notable, however, was the sudden change of heart of Borger who now insisted upon speaking quite favorably of the former President as he now campaigned for the news media's choice for the Oval Office, revealing yet again the hypocrisy that ran rampant through the ranks of the American news media and marked the significant efforts of the Media Political Machine to control the views of voters during the primary elections and leading up to the General Election. This case of flip flopping on the part of the news media also revealed how prone the news media had become to unmatched hypocrisy during the 2008 election that pointed to the existence of the hidden agenda to influence the outcome of the General Election.

2 October 2008

Following the rejection of a $700 billion Wall Street bailout package by the United States House of Representatives, the United States Senate successfully passed the bill a vast majority of Americans saw as a golden parachute for the very institutions responsible for the nation's economic woes. While several agents of the news media chose to simply convey the facts of the mammoth spending bill to viewers eager to gain a better understanding of why the bailout was *needed*, others like CNN's Senior Business Correspondent Ali Velshi chose to report the facts surrounding this issue of national significance in a toxic manner which reflected his support for the bill. Initially, following the request by Bush Administration officials for the multi-billion dollar package to bolster the sagging economy and save the nation's most prominent savings, loans, and investment institutions, several CNN correspondents made a point of reading the emails sent in to broadcasts from viewers expressing staunch opposition to the bill that many viewed as a reward to the nation's leading savings and loans institutions for bad behavior and questionable business practices. Email after email read, reflected strong sentiments from viewers condemning the bill as one that would benefit the rich and leave ordinary working Americans holding the bill. Though every major news network covering the controversial bill reported that the majority of Americans polled regarding the multi-billion dollar Wall Street bailout proposal were undeniably against the bill in any form, following more rhetoric issued by the Bush Administration and the most prominent voices in Congress, including both Senators John McCain and Barack Obama, CNN suddenly squelched the voices of viewers expressing their opposition. CNN correspondents immediately stopped reading the emails of angry viewers expressing heightened concerns regarding the cost of the bill and Ali Velshi said that due to the overwhelming amount of people contacting the network in regards to the bill, that he would host a radio show to entertain the views of Americans regarding the bill. This marked a seemingly deliberate attempt by the network to cease informing viewers of the views of fellow dissenters and opponents of the costly bill. CNN made no attempt to inform viewers of the frequency or channel of the radio station Velshi would conduct his broadcast from nor did the network provide a phone number which could be used to contact Velshi with comments. After the sentiments of the nation's most concerned regarding the issues was successfully hushed by the network through choosing to no longer read or display views opposing the Wall Street bailout package, Velshi reappeared on CNN television broadcasts expressing support for the bill complete with explanations as to why American taxpayers should support it also. Velshi also said the number of Americans contacting him regarding the bill had changed significantly from those who were firmly against it to more people calling in wanting more information regarding the benefits of the bill to the taxpayer. Due to the serious economic issues the majority of Americans were facing at the time, however, it is highly unlikely that any explanation provided would persuade a person against the bill to either want more information regarding the bill that was in excess of $800 billion dollars by the time it passed in the Senate, or persuade someone who was against the bill to now miraculously support it. It is more likely news media entities such as CNN decided once again to completely ignore its duty to keep American society informed through providing facts about an issue of national and international importance to be financed by the American taxpayer, instead choosing to take a position of support for the Wall Street bailout bill to support its own agenda and remain on message with the position of the Media Political Machine's presidential candidate of choice.

It should be noted that Ali Velshi also made an appearance on the "Oprah Winfrey Show" to explain the $700 billion dollar bailout to Winfrey's program viewers in the days leading up to the second vote by the United States House of Representatives regarding the bill.

TOXIC TACTICS:
The Supporting
Viewer Comment

The "Supporting Viewer Comment" in toxic news reporting is one of the most simplistic methods the Media Political Machine uses regularly to persuade viewers to agree or disagree with a certain point of view regarding a given issue. The welcome of viewer comments, in electronic or other forms, by news media correspondents, reporters, or networks is a way to afford program viewers the opportunity to voice their opinions to other viewers by calling in or e-mailing comments to a given news media outlet. In its un-manipulated form, viewer comments provide other program viewers with insight regarding how a viewer feels about popular issues raised by a news network or correspondent. This feedback often provides useful and interesting perspectives that other viewers may not be privy to which, in turn, helps them with the process of assessing an issue. Despite the benefits of exposure to viewer comments and personal opinions regarding a given issue during news media broadcasts, in its toxic form, viewer comments are often used by media outlets to support the perspective of the news media or given correspondent regarding politically charged or highly sensitive issues. The comments submitted by viewers to a given news media outlet take on a toxic nature when they are picked over in the newsroom with only certain or cherry picked comments being selected to be shared with the program's audience. The selected viewer comments most often, conveniently support the opinion of the correspondent and reflect the sentiments that the network is trying to push in an effort to influence its viewers. The submitted viewer comments that support opinions to the contrary are either completely withheld by the correspondent or they are presented in a disproportional manner which makes it seem as if more viewers agree with the expressed opinion of the news correspondent or network. Typically, viewer comments shared with the broadcast audience of a news media program favor the spin presented by the most notorious toxic news correspondents by a margin of three to one.

To safeguard efforts to maintain independent thoughts regarding highly divisive and politically charged issues, viewers should maintain acute awareness that even the most sincere and innocent viewer comments are not immune to manipulation by the Media Political Machine once they reach the newsroom. Though it is unlikely that the Media Political Machine alters the words of written correspondence from viewers, it does, however, frequently opt to share with program viewers only that opinionative viewer correspondence that coincides with network's political platform. These comments should be welcomed by viewers in an open-minded manner, however, viewers must also be careful not to be herded in the direction of the views of toxic news networks and correspondents misusing the sentiments of other viewers to support the spin they peddle in the interest of themselves and the networks that employ them.

6 October 2008

As Senator Barack Obama rocked yet another magazine cover, solo, this time *Men's Vogue*, bringing his total campaign season magazine cover total to nearly thirty, *Newsweek* magazine's October 6 edition featured a shared cover approach with one half of the cover emblazed with a dot matrix image of Barack Obama and the other half, John McCain with the same dot matrix appearance. Senator Obama's half of the magazine cover was a bluish hue, while Senator McCain's half of the cover had a reddish cast. The title stamped on the cover of the magazine read: "Mr. Cool vs. Mr. Hot: How They See the World."[96] The story that coincided with the images on the cover was found on pages twenty-two and twenty-three of the magazine and was written by journalists Jon Meacham and Evan Thomas.

The "Mr. Cool vs. Mr. Hot" story by Meacham and Thomas, as cleverly reinforced by the eye catching magazine cover, briefly yet thoroughly analyzed the dueling personalities of the men involved in one of the most emotionally stirring and hotly contested presidential races in modern American history, with Senator Obama being portrayed as Mr. Cool, and the often allegedly testy Senator McCain being cast as Mr. Hot (headed). At first glance of the cover, it was obvious as to which direction the coinciding story would go: very good for Senator Obama and very bad for Senator McCain. The visual message of the cover stated quite boldly that Senator Obama was a cool, even handed, level headed leader and Senator McCain was obviously a hothead who often acted in a rash and erratic manner even when involved in historical domestic affairs. From the opening lines of the story, it was overwhelmingly evident that *Newsweek* was keeping in step with the Media Political Machine's well orchestrated platform of covering the last candidates standing in an unmistakably biased manner, in efforts to influence its readers to vote for this guy over that one.

Initially asking the question, "how would each man lead,"[97] Meacham and Thomas succeeded in painting a lopsided picture of both candidates, skillfully manipulating the art of word choice and innuendo to disguise the story as wholly objective. Words used to describe Senator Obama in the story included: "precise, occasionally withdrawn, and methodical,"[98] while those used to describe his counterpart included, "passionate, sometimes impulsive, and unpredictable,"[99] as opposed to terms like "experienced" and "seasoned" which would have been more balanced terms casting both in a similar and unbiased light. The more favorable terms used to describe Senator Obama in the story were strikingly similar to the flattering terms used by Time magazine's Joe Klein to describe Obama campaign staffers in a story he penned following Hillary Clinton's party nomination defeat. As for toxic innuendo's, when referring to Senator Obama's involvement in supporting Congress and the Bush Administration in brokering a deal to bail out beleaguered Wall Street entities during the nation's most challenging economic crisis since The Great Depression, Meacham and Thomas wrote on his behalf, "he understood that, by butting into the delicate negotiations between the White House, Treasury and Congress to shape a rescue package, a presidential candidate risked injecting politics and partisanship into a situation that demanded statesmanship and discretion."[100] This statement was a direct reference to Senator McCain's surprising decision to suspend his presidential campaign to "go back to Washington" and do what he could to help broker the deal in his capacity as a U.S. Senator which many saw as nothing more than a stunt to score points with voters and add to his leadership resume during his lackluster presidential campaign.

As skillfully as the CNN and MSNBC News networks repeatedly introduced Senator McCain's age as a major vice in the presidential election of 2008, Meacham and Thomas brought the question of Senator McCain's judgment to the forefront of their argument against McCain, at this point in the campaign season, by pointing to his selection of then Governor Palin as a vice presidential running mate while she was recovering from a widely televised interview with Katie Couric during which she gave several answers that made little sense to even the Joe Six Packs in society. The two *Newsweek* writers further likened Senator McCain's daring, stuntman-like heydays as a Naval pilot to that of his approach to current issues facing American society. Though some of the statements made characterizing McCain were factual and, arguably, justified as in the case of his flip flopping regarding the true state of the economy which

Senator McCain parroted after the Bush Administration as being "fundamentally sound," other statements made about the Senator in the story reflected the intent to make McCain look less appealing than Senator Obama to voters who read it. Immediately following Meacham and Thomas' most critical statements in reference to McCain, statements such as: "Throughout, he was quietly talking to Hank Paulson on a daily basis and grew to like Bush's Treasury secretary so much that he told CNBC he was thinking of keeping him on for at least a transition period,"[101] were made regarding Senator Obama. This particular statement, upon closer inspection, not only spoke favorably in regards to Senator Obama, but also planted the seeds of the inevitability of an Obama presidency. Meacham and Thomas followed up this statement in a few more lines with the statement: "McCain took no position at the meeting, while Obama, at least according to some published accounts, peppered Paulson with questions."[102]

While the authors of the Mr. Cool vs. Mr. Hot story made an attempt at disguising the story as one of balance with its neutral conclusion, it was obvious the intent of the story was issued straight from the presses of the Media Political Machine which used its position, as trusted conveyor of information regarding the last men standing at the door to the Oval Office, to inject toxicity into the political process in favor of Senator Obama over Senator McCain. The words and tactics used to give the Obama campaign an unwarranted helping hand strangely stirred memories of the manner in which the news media handily facilitated the disposal of Senator Clinton during the Democratic primary elections. These actions were also a clear indication that the news media's actions were not at all motivated by partisan politics, but instead the self interest of the Media Political Machine seeking to force Senator Obama into the Office of the President of the United States instead of allowing him to obtain the office on his own merit, which he had already proven he was undoubtedly capable of doing.

There were two irrefutable issues of note surrounding this biased news magazine article. One was that following the painting of a portrait of Senator McCain as "Mr. Hot," a statement was made near the close of the article, that Barry Goldwater was once characterized by Lyndon B. Johnson as someone who was "too hot and could not be trusted with the bomb."[103] This statement was a covert effort to say that Senator McCain could easily be viewed in the same manner—psychologically unstable. Ironically, Goldwater and McCain both hailed from the same state as well. It should also be noted that the terms "cool" and "aloof," both used to describe Senator Obama's demeanor during his debate with Senator McCain in Oxford, Mississippi in this *Newsweek* article, were the exact same terms CNN's Jessica Yellin used to describe Senator Obama during the 5 October broadcast of a recap of the Biden versus Palin debate, hosted by Correspondent John King on CNN. This pointed to a well organized and synchronized effort to sell Senator Obama's immaculate image to the American voter.[104]

8 October 2008

The day following the next to the last debate of the 2008 campaign season between Senators John McCain and Barack Obama, Senator Joe Biden was interviewed on the CBS "Early Show," and Mrs. Obama was interviewed by Larry King on CNN. Interviews featuring Senator John McCain, his wife Cindy, and former Governor Sarah Palin seemed to be none existent on any of the nation's leading news networks save for the FOX News network that was recognized by all to be biased in favor of right wingers despite their slogans attesting to "no spin" and "fair and balanced" reporting. CNN repetitively advertised the Michelle Obama interview days in advance of the presidential debate, but made no mention of a follow up interview featuring Cindy McCain. This despite the news media going out of its way to smear McCain's image by recalling her past issues with drug abuse in several stories featured earlier in the campaign year. CBS News did make mention that then Governor Palin was offered the same opportunity as Senator Biden to be interviewed on the morning show, but also made it a point more than once to inform viewers and voters alike that she declined the offer as if she was somehow obligated to answer the news media's beckon. In addition to featuring Michelle Obama one day after the latest presidential debate, CNN also resurrected the story regarding the health of the candidates with a feature story titled "Fit to Lead"[105] with Sanjay Gupta which was a follow up to the story titled "The First Patient:

Health and the Presidency," that Gupta did a feature on in May of
2008. "The First Patient," insinuated in several ways that Senator
McCain was in no shape to serve as the nation's leader while at the
same time highlighting Senator Obama's youthfulness and clean
bill of health. The advertisements of "Fit to Lead," showed several
graphic pictures of Senator McCain with stitches and wounds
following surgery and treatments for several cases of melanoma.
One advertisement for the version of the story yet to be aired, even
featured a woman who exclaimed, "this is a form of cancer that
kills,"[106] as if genuinely concerned about Senator McCain's health
while simultaneously insinuating he had one foot in the grave and
the other on a banana peel. The latest look at the health of past
Presidents as well as candidates Obama and McCain was scheduled
to be shown on both Saturday and Sunday of the same week.

While the rest of the Media Political Machine was Monday
morning quarterbacking the previous night's debate, and attempting
to sway undecided voters toward Obama using the most biased
forms of reporting in both spoken and written form, the New York
Times was busy serving as an unwarranted and self appointed agent
of the Obama campaign by complaining that the McCain Campaign
was engaging in gutter politics directed at Senator Obama. The truth
of the matter was, though some of the tactics used by a, seemingly,
now desperate McCain Campaign could be considered below the
belt in nature, they seemed liked child's play when compared to the
search and destroy campaign the Media Political Machine waged
against any candidate during the party primaries and leading up to
the General Election that was *not* Senator Barack Obama during the
'08 election season. The New York Times issued its editorial harshly
criticizing the McCain Campaign the day following the October 7
presidential debate, characterizing it as "appalling,"[107] which was
precisely the term many American voters used in political blogs
to characterize the American news media's wrecking crew efforts
to attack the character of several candidates during the elections of
2008. The New York Times, as well as countless other news media
entities seemed to be completely oblivious to the coordinated
attacks made by the news media against Senator Obama's fiercest
opponent during the Democratic Primary elections in which she

was repeatedly characterized in a negative manner and ridiculed openly by leading correspondents and journalists. The *NYT* article came on the heels of a statement made by individuals associated with the McCain Campaign that the news media giant was "an Obama advocacy organization." This was the same accusation leveled at numerous American news media entities during the campaign season, each time being denied by the news media entity it was directed towards and dismissed as nothing more than campaign rhetoric. The problem with the argument, however, was some of the accusations one simply *could not* make up regarding the news media's self interest driven activities during the election season, as in the case of the news media's accusations that former President Clinton was engaging in acts of infidelity while campaigning for Senator Clinton during the primary elections, and that he was a "racist" and had a "nasty temper," which was echoed frequently in many news media forums during Senator Clinton's campaign. Other accusations made by the news media during the Democratic Party primaries included Senator Clinton had "played the race card" during her campaign with a statement made about the demographic breakdown of her supporters versus those of Senator Obama, and that she was engaging in "dirty politics" against Obama any time she verbally challenged or opposed him during the elections. Perhaps the most prominent and lowest forms of media bias during the campaign season was spewed by CNN Correspondent Campbell Brown who, quite often, both openly and flagrantly displayed her contempt for Senator Clinton and the former President while Senator Clinton was in yet in the race for her party's nomination, using extreme insinuation and unprofessional language when referring to the Clintons at a time when some voters were yet undecided about which candidate to support.

While it is possible the statement issued against the *New York Times* by McCain spokesperson Michael Goldfarb that the publisher "obscures its true intentions—to undermine the candidacy of John McCain and boost the candidacy of Barack Obama—under the cloak of objectivity,"[108] may not have been entirely true, it did accurately describe the actions of many of the leading American news media entities during the election season. *NYT* Managing Editor Bill Keller, stated as a rebuttal to the McCain Campaign allegations of bias in favor of Senator Obama that the paper is, "committed to covering the candidates fully, fairly, and aggressively."[109] Goldfarb would have been more accurate to assess the *New York Times* as AWOL at a time in which some major news media entity should have stepped up to the plate to speak out against the presence of bias and lack of objectivity in reporting by the political arm of news media during the election year, much like many of the nation's leading Christian organizations were AWOL during the height of the Civil Rights Movement when it would have done some much good to hear a voice other than that of the oppressed, advocating much needed change. In some cases, not standing up against that that is wrong is just as bad as committing the act itself.

October 2008

The October 13th edition of *Newsweek* magazine featured a cover with a bold, closer than close up shot of Republican vice presidential nominee Sarah Palin. The larger than life sized headshot of Palin was so big that only scarcely more than the left side of her face would even fit on the magazine's cover. At first glance on the newsstand, only Palin's left eye and dangling Alaska shaped gold earring could be made out, because her nose and mouth were covered by a cleverly placed, fold-away flap. Despite this, the part of her face that was exposed was unmistakably Sarah Palin. The very picturesque and photogenic Palin, often jokingly referred to as "Caribou Barbie" was ever the butt of jokes made by the news as well as other media outlets who poked fun at her backwoods Alaskan accent and her folksy manner of public address while stumping for Senator McCain at campaign rallies across the nation. Though it was often hotly debated in Democratic, Republican, and news media circles whether or not Palin "was ready" to be elected to the vice presidency or qualified to be "a heartbeat away" from the office of President, one thing that was not contested was that she was definitely what Southern gentlemen would refer to as "a looker," meaning that she was conspicuously attractive. Palin's physical attractiveness arguably significantly contributed to her appeal to many of her most loyal supporters. Citing this, at first glance of the October '08 *Newsweek* magazine cover, featuring a smiling Palin, the brightly colored depiction of her seemed completely harmless and objective. Only after flipping open the flap that covered Palin's nose and mouth was the news media's latest toxic, yet covert, smear tactic made noticeable. Upon closer inspection of the magnified photograph of Palin's face, the motive behind the proximity of the picture became glaringly obvious, because every imperfection, blemish, and facial hair on Palin's face was, no doubt, purposely put on display for all to see. The magnification of the picture rendered it so defined that the hairs on Palin's upper lip could literally be counted and the same was also true for the, no longer, microscopic hairs on her nose if one had the time to spare. *Newsweek's* effort to display the imperfections on Palin's face, which alluded to likely yet unseen imperfections in her character, was so obvious that several news media television networks featured the magazine on broadcasts, seemingly for the purpose of shedding light on the controversy surrounding the cover, but at the same time, never really coming out and admitting what the problem with the toxic cover was, which in turn, only brought more attention to the cover and stirred the curiosity of many who chose to stop by their local news stand to take a gander. I was included in the number of those who took a gander, finding the underhanded move to highlight the vice presidential candidate's physical imperfections distasteful, unprofessional, and sexist. One only had to research the past covers of *Newsweek* magazine during the course of 2008 to see that the manner in which Palin was portrayed was unprecedented by the publisher and was uncharacteristic of any photograph used for the magazine's cover prior.

The story that corresponded with the uncomplimentary magazine cover featuring Palin was titled "The Palin Problem,"[110] highlighting, quite fairly, issues with the Alaskan Governor and the question of her state of preparedness for the office of the Vice President. Author Jon Meacham, in this case, presented his argument in a very well thought out, researched, and professional manner, using the state of the nation at the time to question what type of leader it was in dire need of, while at the same time drawing attention to then Governor Palin's stump speech comparing herself to a "Joe Six-Pack" kind of politician. While Meacham's argument for taking a closer look at Palin, who seemed to some to have evaded the vetting process prior to selection as Senator McCain's vice presidential running mate, was both compelling, thought provoking, and valid, the publisher's choice to unapologetically display an unflattering picture of Palin on its magazine's cover severely detracted from the objectivity of the message conveyed in the corresponding pages of the magazine by Meacham. The lack of equal treatment displayed by the news media giant when visually depicting Palin on the October 2008 *Newsweek* magazine cover also bordered on sexist in nature and the toxicity exhibited by its poor choice of an approach to voicing apprehension regarding her selection as Senator McCain's running mate, through an emotion and controversy stirring image, went another step further in proving the news media's indisputable bias against those found outside of its favor during the 2008 campaign season.

13 October 2008

CNN decided to *again* air a special report program drawing scrutiny to the health of Senators Obama and McCain as they approached the final stretch of the 2008 General Election. The first version of the story, titled "The First Patient," took a look back at Past Presidents and their often concealed health issues as well as the current state of health of the 2008 contenders for the presidency. "The First Patient" was hosted by the network's Chief Medical Correspondent Dr. Sanjay Gupta and aired only a few short months before the latest presidential contender health condition expose´. The story did Senator McCain no favors, because when boiled down to the bottom line, it drew attention to his age and questioned his fitness to serve in the Oval Office while simultaneously highlighting Senator Obama's youthfulness and clean bill of health.

The version of the analysis of the health of the Democratic and Republican Party nominees for the presidency, titled "Fit to Lead,"[111] that first aired on the network only a week prior, began suggestively, with a clever introduction that referenced the average age that individuals are required to step down or retire from various jobs and positions, citing several examples from the retirement age of a CEO to the mandatory removal date for a senior military officer. The introduction, unmistakably directed at concerns about the age of Senator McCain, was a lead in to Gupta reminding viewers that Senator McCain, if elected, would be the oldest person to ever be elected President of the United States. Just as in the case of "The First Patient," Gupta also reminded viewers that Senator McCain's father died of a stroke at age 70, yet his mother was still very active and quite spry, though in her 90s. Though it was pointed out that Senator McCain was given a clean bill of health by his private physician, Dr. John Eckstein, the story recounted McCain's days as a prisoner of war and made much ado about McCain's resulting physical limitations to include the fact that he walks with a limp and cannot raise his arms above is shoulder. The purpose of highlighting of these limitations seemed to be to make McCain look like a cripple who may not present the image of health that the next leader of the free world is expected to.

After the stage was set with another CNN special report story focused on the health of U.S. President's past as well as that of the 2008 contenders, again casting Senator McCain in an unfavorable light, Gupta and a group of individuals with medical backgrounds poured over 1100 pages of the last eight years of Senator McCain's medical history. Merely the stating of the number of pages of medical documentation McCain had accumulated over the past eight years was enough to cast doubt in the minds of decided and undecided voters alike that the senior politician may have more medical issues than met the eye. This was, no doubt, the desired effect. As if making these negative insinuations in regards to the state of Senator McCain's health was not enough, much reference was made to the 4 melanomas that were removed from the senator's face over the course of several years complete with graphic pictures of McCain immediately following surgery in his scarred and swollen state making him seem both feeble and medically vulnerable. Gupta then informed viewers that 2,768 doctors ran an ad in the New York Times requesting full disclosure of Senator McCain's entire medical file to determine whether or not he would even be able to "complete a full term" in office if elected President. Shortly thereafter, a clip of footage was played showing Senator McCain making a gaffe during a press conference while on a trip abroad, seeming somewhat confused and mistaking Iran for Iraq during his dialogue.

Immediately after the segment of the story that clandestinely raised many issues and questions about Senator McCain's health that were seemingly left unanswered and open ended, leaving the

impression of a McCain presidency being a leap of faith, the half
of the program devoted to the health status of Senator Obama
began with Obama being cited as one of the youngest nominees
of an American political party. Only John F. Kennedy and Bill
Clinton were younger. Correspondent Candy Crowley, who often
provided her openly biased opinions during the election season,
made an appearance on the special and interjected that Senator
Obama regularly made time for exercise even during his campaign
for the presidency. It was then pointed out by Gupta that Senator
Obama used to smoke cigarettes, but had kicked the habit and used
Nicorette gum to help with his efforts to remain smoke free. With
this, Gupta gave the opinion that Senator Obama could be expected
to live up to 32 more years, to approximately the ripe age of 80.[112]
Whether intended or not, this statement also suggested that Senator
McCain at the age of 73, was not far off the mark from a date with
death if the same was the case for him. This would automatically
lead anyone concerned about McCain's fitness to serve, to wonder
if he would be able to complete one term in office, much less two
that would see him to the age of 81 if it came to fruition. While it
was revealed during the program that both Senator Obama's mother
and grandfather died of two very different forms of cancer, Gupta
made the point that neither of these cases left the senator susceptible
to developing cancer himself. Gupta reported that Senator Obama's
private physician had issued the statement that Senator Obama had
no medical issues that would prevent him from serving as President
and showed a one page statement attesting to the Senator's clean
bill of health. The conclusion to the segment of the story focused
on the state of Senator Obama's health yielded a trademark CNN
independent poll that informed viewers that 47% of those polled
said they had a concern regarding Senator McCain's health and
fitness to serve versus 19% that expressed the same concern for
the health of Senator Obama. Dr. Gupta ended the segment with
a look at mental health issues and the presidency being taboo for
past candidates seeking the Oval Office. This segment of the story
indirectly made reference to both Senator John McCain's mental
state as it related to his age, and his mental state resulting from his
experiences as a Prisoner of War. This was an issue that surfaced
several times in McCain's history as a candidate for the presidency

with both President George W. Bush and Senator Obama making references to the state of McCain's "bearings" while facing him as an opponent.

14 October 2008

Newsmax.com, often credited as the leading online news source for conservatives, at times referenced by Rush Limbaugh on his popular conservative radio talk show, published the October 2008 edition of its magazine with the picture of a headless agent of the news media, in a suit, holding a framed picture. The picture proudly held by the mock member of the press, as indicated by the brightly colored "press" button pinned to his lapel, was of none other than that of a smiling Senator Barack Obama. Written in varied handwriting styles on the picture, mockingly made for presentation to Senator Obama, were the following statements: "Loved our special time in Iowa—CNN." "Dear B—What would we do without you?—*Newsweek*." "Thanks for everything!—MSNBC." "Let's set up another cover story **SOON**!—*Time*." The magazine cover's corresponding story was titled "Media's Love Affair With Barack Obama." Though the magazine was unquestionably biased in favor of the views of its conservative base, as evidenced by the contents of articles and editorials found throughout, what was interesting about the October edition's cover art was the fact that each of the mock signers of the Obama portrait, CNN, *Newsweek*, *Time*, and MSNBC were precisely the usual suspects of the news media that both brazenly and repeatedly displayed undeniable bias in favor of Senator Obama during the 2008 election season. Though there were countless other agents of the mainstream news media, thoroughly documented, that also provided coverage of the presidential race in a toxic manner, openly showing favor for Senator Obama over all other candidates during the election season, the four juggernauts of the American news media, dimed out by *Newsmax* magazine on the cover of its October 2008 edition, reigned supreme as the least objective providers of news surrounding the elections during perhaps the most critical campaign of our lifetime, confirming my own suspicions of their ill intent.

"Love At First Sight,"[113] by Eric Deggans, was the coinciding story found on pages 56 through 64 of the magazine, providing an opinion regarding the biased coverage of the campaigns leading up to the General Election, as seen through the eyes of conservatives. The story was visually prefaced, on its opening pages, by the picture of an old brown medicine bottle with the image of Senator McCain on the side and the words "old fashioned" stamped underneath sitting behind and to the left of a family sized, brightly colored detergent bottle with a picture of the beaming face of Barack Obama with the words, "new" and "all new" plastered on it wherever there was space. Though these depictions of the images of the presidential candidates were a highly exaggerated attempt at poking fun at how the American news media consistently portrayed the two on broadcasts and in various news media publications, it accurately described, without words, the easily demonstrable bias that plagued news media outlets and coverage of the election season.

Deggans opened the story with an interesting account of outspoken conservative and FOX News analyst, Juan Williams, witnessing at Obama rallies, during the Democratic primaries, the presence of some of the most prominent news media editors and executives. Williams found the presence of these individuals puzzling because they were not there for purposes of covering the campaign for their various news media entities. Instead, Williams recounted, after speaking with them, he learned that they felt that history was in the making and they wanted to be a part of it. This occurrence took place during the infancy of the 2008 Democratic primary process, even as early as the Iowa and New Hampshire primaries. After the witnessing of the brazen news media bias during the campaign season that followed, it now strangely seemed that not only was the news media interested in being a part of history in the making, but was also not above facilitating or forcing its coming to pass, partially explaining its inclination to favor Senator Obama throughout the election season while going out of its way to ignore or demonize each of his most competitive opponents in a manner so extreme that it undoubtedly had an adverse effect on their campaign efforts.

Throughout the *Newsmax* story, Deggans cited several studies that pointed to unequivocal bias on the part of the news media during the elections to include one conducted by the Project for Excellence in Journalism that attested to its occurrence after monitoring some 48 news outlets per week. Deggans also cited a reliable source at the *Washington Post* who confirmed that, regarding the newspaper's coverage of the campaigns leading up to the General Election, it published 142 stories about Senator Obama versus 96 about Senator McCain. The numbers in regards to photographs of the two candidates put into print by the newspaper yielded roughly the same average. When Deggans asked agents of the news media why the coverage of the campaigns was so lopsided, they responded that there was less known about national political newcomer, Obama, and it was simply "the nature of journalism to run around and pay a lot of attention to whatever is new."[114] While this may have been adequate enough, in the minds of news media agents, to explain away the bias they exhibited during the campaigns, it did not explain why they often presented candidates that were opponents of Senator Obama in such an overwhelmingly negative manner. While Deggans did not spend much time dissecting how media negativity directed at candidates affected the balance of the coverage of the 2008 elections, he did cite the findings of the right leaning Media Research Center that indicated Obama's dominating press coverage by the news media had a significant impact on his win over Hillary Clinton for the Democratic nomination. Deggans also pointed out the MRC additionally found that three prominent news networks ran 462 stories that could be considered positive for Senator Obama compared to only 70 stories that could be considered negative about him. While the study was not without its flaws as pointed out by Deggans who also cited the sentiments of critics of the study, and though the study was conducted by an admittedly conservative research organization, it did however address the sentiments of many observers that a Media Political Machine existed and had succeeded in having an unfair influence on the '08 elections.

The balance of Deggans' well written and analytical story focused on the massive loss of credibility of leading American news media outlets due to their unequivocal bias in coverage of the 2008 campaigns and elections. The section of the story found on page 62 of the magazine prominently displayed eight *Time* magazine covers featuring Senator Obama, all published during the course of the '08 election season, to skillfully drive home this point. Of the dilemma voters faced in 2008, on a daily basis, while attempting to distinguish between serious news reporters and journalists, and those such as Bill O'Reilly, Keith Olbermann, and Chris Matthews who often spewed more opinion than fact when covering the elections, Deggans wrote: "although the complaints about bias are sure to continue, executives at the largest cable news channels have made it clear as long as ratings remain unaffected, the blend between opinion-makers and objective reporters is likely to continue."[115] This statement framed the widespread sentiments of the news media's leading shakers and movers who acknowledged the lack of objectivity in their coverage of the 2008 election season, yet refused to do anything about it as long as ratings and sales remained unaffected, at least in a manner that would cause them to *lose* money.

17 October 2008

With 18 days to go until the General Election, the Media Political Machine kicked its campaign into high gear through repeated reference of poll numbers turned out by every major news media entity as well as every reputable polling organization, all heavily favoring Senator Obama to pull off a win on 4 November. Many states that were Republican strongholds in 2000 and 2004 were now declared "in play" by the news media's leading talking heads and correspondents, and all of them slanted their programs and stories to favor Senator Obama for President. It all strangely mirrored the political posturing by the media during the Democratic Party primary elections, displaying indisputable bias in favor of Obama while openly tolling the bells for the McCain Campaign which it had begun to count out just as it had the Hillary Clinton campaign for the Democratic Party nomination.

17 October brought news of a highly anticipated appearance of former Secretary of State Colin Powell on NBC's "Meet the Press."[116] The news media immediately seized upon the announcement of the guest appearance as an opportunity to plant seeds of a possible surprise endorsement by Powell which many correspondents saw as a possible deal sealer for Senator Obama as they actively sought justification to call the race early for Obama much like it did during the primaries. Colin Powell made no public statement or indication

that could even remotely be translated into a possible endorsement for either Senator Obama or Senator McCain yet the news media once again took the liberty to insinuate that Powell would indeed formally endorse Senator Obama at some point during his "Meet the Press" interview. The insinuation that Powell "might" endorse Senator Obama for the presidency seemed like another attempt by the Media Political Machine to pressure Powell into endorsing Senator Obama roughly two weeks out from the General Election, perhaps giving the Obama campaign the final needed push to bring an Obama presidency to fruition through manipulating a highly respected figure in American conservative politics. The strong arm tactic used by the news media in the precious few days remaining until the General Election was strikingly similar to the method employed to pressure the Clintons into campaigning for Senator Obama following the Democratic primary elections, only in milder form. Through suggesting that Powell "might" endorse Senator Obama, the news media was essentially saying to Powell and voters alike that he "should" formally endorse Senator Obama which, if Powell took note, may have made him feel pressured or compelled to do so. The same was true of former President Clinton when the media repeatedly raised the question regarding "whether the former President was doing enough" to support Senator Obama in his campaign for the presidency following his formal acceptance of the Democratic Party nomination.

The day also brought news of the endorsement of Senator Obama by three "high profile" newspapers, two of which had never endorsed a Democratic presidential candidate in the history of their existence. In the glowing endorsements of the *Chicago Tribune*, *Los Angeles Times*, and *The Washington Post*,[117] Senator Obama was lauded for the skill he exhibited while conducting his presidential campaign. The newspapers further cited the historical nature of Obama's candidacy as the first African American to be nominated to the presidency by a major American political party. The historical nature of Obama's potential to be elected to the Oval Office, now being referenced by pillars of the news media repeatedly, hinted at the presence of a well orchestrated effort to aid Senator Obama in being elected through hyper-exposure using favorable news coverage, consecutive cover stories by leading publishers, glowing

media endorsements, and negative coverage of the opposition—
often times literally.

19 October 2008

The news media was much abuzz during early morning
broadcasts and the taping of NBC's "Meet the Press," featuring
former Secretary of State Colin Powell. Under the title of "breaking
news" that had long since become a tool the news media used to
add hype to its programs instead of to announce actual newsworthy
facts of an urgent nature, program viewers awakened to news media
broadcasts anticipating the formal endorsement of Senator Obama
for the presidency by Powell, a core loyalist of the Republican Party
and longtime friend of Senator John McCain. When the awaited
news that Powell had indeed formally endorsed Senator Obama
during the recording of "Meet the Press" arrived, leading news media
networks gleefully reported the news even before the show could be
aired. Though it could not be argued or doubted that this was a major
endorsement that could lend even more credibility to the Obama case
for the presidency, the media conveniently refrained from any form
of criticism regarding the motives and timing of the endorsement
roughly two weeks out from the General Election. The news media
that prided itself with asking the "hard questions" and placing
viewers in the "no spin zone" through employing "no bias, no bull"
reporting tactics, in the midst of its celebration, felt it unnecessary
to analyze the endorsement in depth in regards to what was in it for
Powell, the way it scrutinized stories regarding the endorsement of
other candidates throughout the campaign season. Had the Media
Political Machine chosen to be objective regarding the endorsement,
it may have raised issues for discussion such as why Powell waited so
long to endorse Senator Obama for the presidency or whether or not
his endorsement had anything to do with his being portrayed as a top
advocate for initiating a war with Iraq on the world stage as well as
in Oliver Stone's movie "W" which reflected unflatteringly upon his
character and was released only two days prior to his endorsement.
More directly, was Powell's endorsement a genuine, selfless stamp of
approval for a candidate that, for most of the campaign season, he
refused to acknowledge support for, or was it an attempt to redeem

himself for the regrettable act of making the case against Iraq to the United Nations that eventually led to the U.S. invasion of the sovereign nation based on faulty intelligence? Powell was not asked the tough questions regarding his eleventh hour endorsement, and for the sake of balance, was not scrutinized or criticized regarding his announcement in the manner that many others were during the election season. The double standard in covering the announcement that lent enormous credibility to Senator Obama as a leader following the news media's repeated efforts to minimize the effects of such announcements favoring other candidates throughout the election season served as key evidence that the political arm of the news media was engaged in its own campaign to influence the outcome of the General Election in favor of its choice for the presidency.

23 October 2008

As a last ditch effort to sway voters in favor of Senator Barack Obama in the waning weeks before the General Election, the Media Political Machine stooped to an all new low through the employment of scare tactics during a network broadcast. As skillfully as the Bush Administration used the words "terrorist," "Al Qaeda," and "Bin Laden," to stir fear and trepidation in the hearts of Americans whenever the President's approval ratings began to plummet or whenever the Democrats seemed to be gaining too much ground, leading our citizens to wonder if their next door neighbors could be Al Qaeda operatives, CNN's Rick Sanchez cranked up the American news media's terror mill in an effort to scare viewers into voting for Senator Obama in the General Election. Sanchez, whose trademark exaggerated mannerisms and dramatics added to the effect of the stories he presented, introduced a story on the midday broadcast regarding a mystery Website, said to have been posted and maintained by Al Qaeda, that actually weighed in on the organization's choice for the next President of the United States. Sanchez seemed to take pride in reporting on the organization's choice, as if it should have really mattered to Americans who Al Qaeda favored to succeed President George W. Bush in the Oval Office. Supported by panel members, including writer Richard Clarke, CNN Security Analyst Mike Brooks, and CNN Justice Correspondent Kelli Arena, Sanchez reported that a statement made on the mystery Website indicated that Al Qaeda was, surprisingly, in support of John McCain, because the organization allegedly asserted that it could be sure he would carry out more attacks on Al Qaeda that would lead to the depletion of America's resources in an already unstable economy.[118] By presenting this argument, Sanchez and CNN cleverly planted seeds of deceit that could have led some to be swayed by fear of giving Al Qaeda what it allegedly wanted—a McCain victory. One problem with the story, however, was that Sanchez refused to reveal the Website address, "due to security concerns," so the possibility of viewers performing an independent fact check of the report was not possible. Additionally, the panel members presented absolutely no arguments disputing the report nor made the suggestion that the true wishes of Al Qaeda could actually be the reverse. Arguments that could have been presented for the sake of balance included the organization may have favored an Obama victory because he was new and in some regards untested, because he was thought by some to have Islamic roots, and because John McCain, like President Bush would likely not hesitate to strike the organization preemptively and decisively to protect American citizens, possibly rendering the organization completely inoperable. Senator Obama would undoubtedly do the same if faced with a situation in which the country's national security was threatened, however there was no doubt that Al Qaeda knew all too well what George W. Bush Republicans meant for their efforts and operations.

Whatever the case was with the preference of the terrorist organization regarding the presidential election, it was all too obvious that since the Website address was not revealed and the panel presented no arguments challenging Sanchez's report, the story was geared toward making Senator McCain look less attractive as a choice for the presidency through fear mongering which was clearly an effort by the political arm of the media to favor Senator Obama over Senator McCain.

26 October 2008

With nine days to go until the General Election and the campaign efforts of the Media Political Machine in full swing, CBSNews.com, though subtly, continued its participation in the concerted efforts of the American news media to influence the election's outcome. On the network's Website listed under the heading and subheading "Inside CBSNews.com," and "Politics," three headlines were listed in a manner that clandestinely reflected favorably on Senator Obama while presenting Senator McCain in a not so favorable manner and arguably brought the integrity of the McCain-Palin Campaign into question. The headlines for the politics section on the Website read, in order, as follows: "Obama rallies Supporters In Colorado;" "McCain 1/3 Palin Clothes Already Returned," "Web Campaign Donations Face Scrutiny." The headline about Senator McCain was in direct reference to a controversy stirred by the news media regarding an alleged expenditure of $150,000 by the Republican National Committee on clothes for former Governor Palin to be worn during the remainder of the campaign. The news media used the story to sustain its assault on Senator Obama's opposition in efforts to smear the McCain-Palin ticket while serving as a pep squad for Senators Obama and Biden.

While the opening line of the story regarding Obama's Colorado campaign rally read, "Barack Obama presided over a Colorado rally so enormous and energetic that even he seemed surprised at his following,"[119] and made reference to the attendance of over 100,000 people who braved the chilly temperature to hear him speak that day, the story regarding Senator McCain opened on a much less positive note. Instead of prefacing the story with information regarding Senator McCain's guest appearance earlier in the morning on NBC's "Meet the Press," or covering his campaign rally in Iowa later in the day, as in the case of the story written regarding Senator Obama, McCain's story purposely began with controversy. "Republican John McCain said Sunday that one-third of the $150,000 that the GOP spent on clothing and accessories for his running mate, Alaska Gov. Sarah Palin, and family, is given back,"[120] was the opening line of the story. If CBS had chosen to write the story regarding McCain in a more objective manner, the story would have read a little more like the story written about Obama, which began with backdrop information and focused upon his campaign speech as well as background information about the state and the significance of the campaign stop. Instead, the story about Senator McCain, who made a campaign stop in Waterloo, Iowa following his "Meet the Press" interview, focused entirely on the silly and meaningless controversy regarding Palin's clothes.

With the stories placed side by side, it became even more apparent that news media bias in coverage of the final days of the campaign season had infested almost every outlet of the press and heavily favored Senator Obama for the presidency. While there were many easily detected infractions in the stories that pointed to the injection of toxicity into the conveying of factual newsworthy information regarding the two candidates on this day, there were a few that could absolutely not be ignored due to blatant, in your face bias geared toward making one candidate look good while making the other look questionable. The first thing that pointed to the existence of bias in presenting the stories together on the network's website was the fact that the Associated Press was the only source credited for the Obama story while the McCain story gave credit to both the network (CBS) and the Associated Press. This led to the suspicion that the story was altered from its previous state and re-written by an agent of the network in a more negative manner. The second thing that indicated the presence of bias in the stories was that in the story about Obama, several references were made to the size of the crowd that came out to support him at the campaign stop. "Do you ever have small crowds in Denver?"[121] a smiling Obama inquired, was one of the quotes used following statements that placed the size of the crowd between 75,000 and "well over" 100,000 people. No reference was made to the size of the crowd that came out in Iowa in support of John McCain. Finally, quotes were lifted from Obama's speech to the crowd gathered at his campaign stop in Colorado that day, including barbs leveled at Senator McCain in reference to statements he made during the campaign. All quotes in the story about Senator McCain on the same day were limited to his responses to questions about the inane Palin wardrobe controversy. No quotes were referenced in regards to the message McCain delivered while on the stump at his campaign stop. The following quotes were used, in closing, for each of the stories respectively. "Obama released a new TV ad Sunday that describes McCain as Obama often does on the campaign trail – as out of ideas, out of touch, and running out of time. It also says McCain is resorting to smears and scare tactics because he doesn't have a plan to fix the economy. The 30-second add will begin running Monday on national cable television outlets."[122] "With just nine days to go before the Nov. 4 election, Palin was making another push in the swing state of Florida, where most polls show Obama leading McCain."[123]

27 October 2008

At the point of there being only being eight days left until the General Election the news media began to frequently employ the exact same tactics on Senator McCain as it did on Senator Clinton during the Democratic Party primary elections. With early voting well under way and only days left to go in the campaign season, the Media Political Machine pulled out all the stops and political rhetoric to convince viewers that due to recent poll results from various sources, including *The Washington Post*, CNN, MSNBC, and *Newsweek* magazine, Senator McCain had absolutely no chance of winning the presidential election and Senator Obama would likely win by a landslide. In addition to this, the news broke that an "unnamed source" associated with the McCain-Palin Campaign said that the campaign was subject to infighting and disorganization, which was ironically the same accusation made by unnamed sources within the Hillary Clinton campaign regarding unrest in its ranks. If the information regarding the campaign was indeed credible, it no doubt was leaked to one of the news media's many embedded correspondents that, during the 2008 elections, proved to be just as detrimental as helpful in regards to providing up to the minute information from a campaign insider's point of view. In several cases, correspondent embeds, instead of providing factual information regarding campaign and candidate activities in an objective manner, slinked around, waiting from some weak and disloyal campaign worker (who probably never read "Stickin'") to feed them some dirt with which they joyfully ran with and used against the very campaign with which they were embedded. The only exception to this was in the case of the campaigns that died on the vine early, and the Obama campaign who had loyalists like Suzanne Malveuax, once a Bush Administration cheerleader, now on the Obama band wagon, who exhibited the loyalty of some of the Senator's most trusted advisors, drumming up support through overly favorable and doting coverage, like a well paid blues performer's front man.

Throughout the day, while it was quite easy to find broadcasts "measuring the drapes" for Senator Obama's presidency, traces of any positive press coverage for Senator McCain was nil because the media continued to seize upon the Palin wardrobe controversy, keeping it fresh on the minds of viewers through repetitive reference, while simultaneously limiting coverage of McCain Campaign stops and activities. MSNBC Chief Washington Correspondent Nora O'Donnell, continued beating the Palin wardrobe horse on her midday interview of then Republican National Convention Chairman, Mike Duncan. Though Duncan tried several times to address political issues far more important to American voters and program viewers such as differences in McCain and Obama tax plans, as well as Republican vulnerabilities in upcoming congressional elections, O'Donnell unremittingly badgered him regarding the idiocy of who was responsible for then Governor Palin spending $150,000 on a new wardrobe for herself and her family during the campaign season. Even after Duncan answered the question by saying the RNC both authorized and bankrolled the purchase, O'Donnell refused to let Duncan move on to other issues until he answered the question in a manner acceptable to her as if she had the authority of a congressional ethics committee chairman in a corruption hearing. In sharp contrast to her interview with Duncan, O'Donnell tossed softball questions to then Democratic National Committee Chairman Howard Dean. She did mockingly ask Dean if the DNC paid for ties for Senators Obama and Biden, because she snapped back at Duncan, during his earlier interview, that she would do so when he suggested she grill the DNC about the issue of campaign clothing purchases in the same manner that she did him. O'Donnell's boldness in acting in an unprofessional and condescending manner while interviewing the chairman of the RNC reflected the same flagrance that had become commonplace in the ranks of the national news media and represented a flexing of the muscles of the Media Political Machine that had successfully wrecked the campaigns of the opposition during the 2008 elections and was on its way to declaring victory for itself in the General Election.

The remainder of the day's MSNBC news broadcast titled, "The Final Stretch," amounted to more campaigning by the news media against the McCain-Palin Campaign. A puppet panel all but wrote the campaign off as a complete loss while insisting that Palin was not qualified to serve as the country's Vice President and was now a bigger drag on McCain than even George W. Bush with his 26% or lower approval rating. Several more references were made to the cost of Palin's wardrobe in a manner that smacked of sexism and the intent to keep the fire burning regarding the controversial topic. MSNBC's "Race For the White House" Correspondent David Gregory, who initially came on board as more impartial than expelled co-hosts Keith Olbermann and Chris Matthews, interviewed McCain Senior Advisor Nicolle Wallace and suggestively asked her a leading question regarding what Senator McCain would do *when* he did not win. He followed up the question with a similar one as to whether McCain would consider working in an Obama Administration, insinuating that McCain should consider what his next line of work would be *when* he lost the General Election.

"Hardball with Chris Matthews" yielded no different or less biased point of view with Matthews linking the conviction of the senior most Republican Senator Ted Stevens on seven counts of corruption to the McCain-Palin Campaign. Matthews was careful to remind viewers and voters that Stevens hailed from the state of Alaska seemingly in efforts to draw a link between the character of former Governor Palin and the now tarnished reputation of a fellow native politician from the state of Alaska. It was also stressed during the program and many times throughout the evening that Senator Obama's latest stump speech was the "closing argument" for his presidential campaign, covertly insinuating that the 2008 General Election was all but in a "case closed" status in favor of an Obama victory.

TOXIC TACTICS:
The Leading Question

The "Leading Question" was a method employed most often during the 2008 elections by news media correspondents that sought to inject toxicity into broadcasts or programs while at the same time portraying the image of an impartial and objective agent of the news media during a time when most correspondents and journalists did not even attempt to hide their unfettered bias. This highly effective means of conveying toxic information was used by only the most skilled news media correspondents, dead set on showing loyalty to the Media Political Machine while simultaneously protecting his or her own image, masquerading as one of the few remaining fair and balanced news media agents in existence. While a quite simplistic means of throwing a rock and hiding a hand, this toxic tactic was used both frequently and skillfully by the likes of "CNN 360" host, Correspondent Anderson Cooper who quizzed program guests with the precision of a seasoned defense attorney, picking apart the case of the prosecution. Before the prosecutor could utter the word "objection," however, on the heels of a question asked in a manner to "lead" or insinuate, the litigator, Cooper in this case, skillfully left it on the table for a collaborator or unsuspecting guest to run with. Here is an example. A non-toxic question would go as follows: "What do you think about the Obama tax plan versus that of Senator McCain?" In sharp contrast, a toxic or leading question would go like this: "Don't you think the McCain tax plan gives too much of a break to the portion of our population making over $250,000?" Another example in non-toxic form would be: "What are some major issues that you see as being a drag on the Obama and the McCain campaigns at the present time?" Again, a toxic and leading question would be similar to the following: "Isn't Sarah Palin proving to be a drag on the McCain campaign whereby she once seemed to re-energize the Republican base's enthusiasm for a John McCain presidency?"

While many cable news media correspondents displayed overt bias in reporting and broadcasts during the 2008 campaign season, many correspondents used leading questions to inflict just as much damage to campaigns counter to that of Senator Obama's as those who were brazenly critical of and openly biased toward them. This toxic news reporting tactic was highly damaging in nature to those candidates and campaigns on the receiving end of such a manner of questioning. What was just as damaging, was the unfair manner in which the tactic was used against select campaigns, but not others. This toxic tactic proved to be one of the most frequently used and effective methods by which agents of the news media injected toxic opinions and ideas into news programming while attempting to seem fair and balanced in delivery. The most effective safeguard against the noxious rhetoric introduced by the "leading question" toxic news reporting tactic is to be wary of feedback from news media broadcast guests that are the result of questions fielded that insinuate or plant ideas through the manner in which they are asked.

29 October 2008

While the *New Mexico Sun Times*[124] was rolling the presses on its premature election edition headline, "Obama Wins," making the claim that it was a bi-monthly newspaper and its October 26 to November 8 edition *had* to be printed in this manner based on an overwhelming lead by Obama in the polls and the next edition not being due until after the General Election, Politico.com was on the defensive, attempting to explain away the fact of the news media's unequivocal bias spanning the entire '08 election season. In a story found on its Website titled, "Why McCain Is Getting Hosed In the Press,"[125] written by John F. Harris and Jim VandeHei, a ridiculously lame case was laid out as to why McCain was receiving almost entirely negative coverage by major news media entities while Senator Obama was receiving the opposite. In the opening lines of the story, the two authors admitted that the reason for them addressing the widely complained about issue was due to hate mail received, admonishing them for explicit bias favoring Senator Obama detected in stories originating from the political Website. Harris and Vandehei then cited the findings of the Project for Excellence in Journalism, stating the obvious regarding overwhelmingly positive coverage by the news media for Senator Obama versus overwhelmingly negative coverage by the news media for Senator McCain throughout the campaign season. It was obvious that this was no surprise to the authors since their employer was among the worst offenders during the latter days of the election season and seemingly on board with the mission of the Media Political Machine during the elections. "OK, let's just get this over with: Yes, in the closing weeks of this election, John McCain and Sarah Palin are getting hosed in the press, and at Politico,"[126] the authors wrote. They went on however, to justify the overwhelming bias in coverage favoring one candidate over all others by essentially stating that the news media coverage of the election season only *seemed* to be biased to those who harbored acute biases of their own. What?! Is that to say, we know we have covered the elections in an unprecedented grossly biased manner, but you are biased too because you noticed we were doing so? The story went on in an attempt to explain away the news media's toxic partiality by stating, regarding the two campaigns, that "McCain's campaign is going quite poorly and Obama's is going well. Imposing artificial balance on this reality would be a bias of its own."[127] This amounted to nothing more than a lame excuse for the news media's wrongdoing during the campaign, because much of the blame for the poor performance of more than one political campaign of 2008 could be directly attributed to the facilitation of its troubles by the news media and the aggressively negative coverage it inflicted upon those of its choosing. Additionally, Harris and VandeHei also refrained from pointing out the fact that the news media went out of its way to accentuate the negative in certain campaigns, including McCain's while completely ignoring the positive in regards to the same. The exact inverse was practiced in the case of Senator Obama and his campaign.

Politico.com, in the spirit of objectivity, conducted an independent investigation of the nature of coverage it provided to the Obama and McCain Campaigns in the days following the party nominations, which not surprisingly, yielded the same conclusion as the study conducted by the Project for Excellence in Journalism. Despite this, unfortunately, the authors of this story tried to use some convoluted, rhetorical, psychologically based BS to insist that most journalists are not inclined to bias because of their strong sense of dedication to being professional stewards of their craft. "The main reason is that for most journalists, professional obligations trump personal preferences. Most political reporters are temperamentally inclined to see multiple sides of a story, and being detached from their own opinions comes relatively easy,"[128] they wrote. This statement was either evidence that Harris and VandeHei were both cryogenically incapacitated during the 2008 campaign season or they did not mind lying in attempts to salvage the integrity of the American news media at a time when, what was left of it was in ruins.

The final page or so of "Why McCain is getting hosed by the press," laid the groundwork for several supporting excuses as to why it *seemed like* the news media's coverage of the campaigns was so biased. Included in these was the argument that Obama somehow benefitted from being an African American and was not subject to certain forms of scrutiny during the campaign because it would "carry an out of bounds racial subtext."[129] The authors also wrote, "In addition, Obama has benefitted from his ability to minimize internal drama and maximize secrecy—and thus to starve feed the press' bias for palace intrigue."[130] Contrary to this point, however, it seemed more likely the efforts of the press to squelch negative coverage of the Obama campaign explained why there was never a mention of disorganization or political infighting associated with it. As for the Clinton and McCain Campaigns, which provided the fiercest competition for the Illinois Senator, media embeds, no doubt facilitated the leakage of negative information regarding campaign inner workings that can no doubt be found in any organization of its magnitude if one looked hard enough. The bottom line was, the choice to exploit the negative versus accentuate the positive regarding the campaigns was solely the choice of the news media, so if there was anything negative associated with the inner workings of the Obama campaign, it would not take a nuclear physicist to understand why viewers were never made aware of it. Still another argument made by the authors to justify the toxicity associated with coverage of the campaigns was that the "momentum" favored Senator Obama. "A candidate who is perceived to be doing well tends to get even more positive coverage (about his or her big crowds or latest favorable polls or whatever),"[131] they wrote. The unfortunate thing about this statement, however, was that with so much off center bias in the ranks of the news media during the campaigns, how could the media be trusted to accurately report who, in fact, the momentum favored?

Though the hosing of McCain by the news media story was a good attempt at clearing the name of the rogue entity entrusted with keeping our nation's citizens informed through unbiased coverage of newsworthy events, it fell far short of convincing. While the story was packed with excuses as to why the travesty of overwhelmingly biased news coverage occurred during the elections, there was no trace of remorse or sense of responsibility for its undertaking—even after admitting to its taking place. The two Politico journalists did however make a last ditch effort to turn the tables on criticism of biased news media coverage by stating: "Then there is bend-over-backward bias. This is when journalists try so hard to avoid accusations of favoritism that it clouds critical judgment."[132] The unfortunate thing was this was not at all applicable to the situation at hand and was almost never the case during the entirety of 2008 election season. Though Harris and VandeHei completely steered clear of addressing the possible effects of the existence of unbridled news media bias during the 2008 primary elections and in the weeks leading up to the General Election, *Augusta Chronicle* political cartoonist, Rick McKee hit the nail on the head with his October 26 political illustration.

"Tonight: Gosh What Could Possibly Be the Cause of Sarah Palin's Falling Poll Numbers?"

31 October 2008

By this time it was obvious, even to the American news media itself, the nation's respect for and trust in the press had gone the way of the reverence for anything Republican after the presidency of George W. Bush—with the wind. Though the agents of the Media Political Machine were getting in the last licks against the McCain Campaign, much work was needed in the area of regaining the respect of the nation's citizens following a long list of infractions during the 2008 elections that compromised the integrity of the news media, be it in network broadcast or published form. It seemed that there was no shortage of e-mails, letters, and phone calls to various news media entities in which the public's displeasure for the overtly biased coverage of the election season were explicitly expressed. As a result of this, there was a surge in attempts by the news media to explain away its countless documented toxic misdeeds geared toward significantly impacting the General Election's outcome just before the November 4 showdown.

As cable news networks remained in the tank for an Obama General Election victory, the news media simultaneously stepped up efforts to repair its badly damaged reputation, which it had, not so long ago, traded for political gain and influence. Many of these efforts came in written form, designed for news media junkies to stumble across accidently so as not to bring too much attention to news media's subtle admission of guilt. Politico, published one such story aimed at addressing the issue of the news media's pick and choose attitude toward following leads on stories that could possibly derail candidates' campaign efforts during the '08 elections. The story opened much like the Politico's story regarding why Senator McCain was being trashed by the news media in that it cited the recent influx of several emails and letters to editors regarding the *perceived* bias of the American news media, as a collective, which often displayed characteristics of being an extension of the Barack Obama campaign for the presidency. Contributors to the story included Avi Zenilman, David Paul Kuhn, Kenneth P. Vogel, and Charles Mahtesian, all from Politico. The story seemed to be motivated by accusations from the McCain Campaign regarding the *Los Angeles Times'* refusal to release a video said to contain footage of Senator Obama hobnobbing with Rashid Khalidi, a Palestinian-American professor and critic of Israel at a party thrown for the Columbia University educator in 2003. Because of alleged ties to the Palestinian Liberation Organization and engaging in public criticism of Israel, an American ally, anything more than a casual relationship between Khalidi and the General Election poll front-runner Obama, could prove critical to an Obama victory in November. What was more was that 1960's radical Bill Ayers was also alleged to have been in attendance at the event documented on the video held by the *Los Angeles Times*.

The newspaper quickly defended itself, citing its publishing of a detailed account of what was on the video, some six months earlier. The newspaper then refused to release the video tape because of an alleged promise made to its supplier that it would not do so. It should be noted that the *Los Angeles Times* had, only weeks before, endorsed Senator Obama for the presidency and it is doubtful that the newspaper would have any interest in bringing the Senator's character into question after its glowing endorsement of him only days out from the General Election—so much for objectivity. This would also mark a complete about face from the news media's damage control efforts it frequently employed on behalf of Senator Obama's campaign at the same time it went out of its way to highlight the negative in the campaigns of other candidates during the 2008 elections. Another issue of note is the fact that a link between Senator McCain and Khalidi had also been uncovered after it was revealed that fifteen years ago, The Center for Palestine Research and Studies, an organization co-founded by Khalidi, received almost a half million dollars from an organization chaired by McCain.

In regards to the Khalidi tapes controversy, another Politico story, "Cover This! Inside Nastiest '08 Rumors,"[133] went the typical route of agents of the news media, when accused of bias during the campaign season, blaming everyone else for the lack of objectivity in news reports and publications covering the elections. It attributed requests by the McCain Campaign that the video in question be released, to the campaign's belief that, "the Times missed, or concealed, some explosive element when it broke the story of the tape."[134] The newspaper also concluded that the motivation behind the request for the release of the video was "driven by some of the same longings for political kryptonite."[135] Whether the assertion leveled by the McCain Campaign was true or not that the *Times* was holding back on the contents of the Khalidi video, because of the serious deficiency of integrity in the news media at the time, the newspaper's choice to keep the actual footage of the tape close hold, only served to fan the flames of suspicion that the campaign of the Media Political Machine ran parallel to that of the Obama campaign for the presidency, and counter to all others.

Politico's rumor '08 story further attempted to tackle the reason for the news media's hesitance to cover some stories that could cast the two most prominent remaining contenders for the presidency during the campaign season in a less than favorable light. It contended that most of the requests to investigate stories of a scandalous nature that flowed in to the news rooms were calls to investigate issues about Senator Obama, according to the findings of the nonpartisan Annenberg Political Fact Check. The story further explained that most of the requests came at a time when Senator Obama built new leads in the polls, making a clear link to partisan politics. Politico's story went on to tell about many of the stories that brought into question the character of both Senators Obama and McCain, and were either debunked following news media investigations or not investigated due to lack of sufficient evidence that there was anything there. The story's author, if not solely the agents of Politico named earlier, wasted no time in blaming the requests for further investigation into the authenticity of Senator Obama's citizenship on the Hillary Clinton campaign for the Democratic Party nomination. Other allegations that enquiring minds called for further insight regarding included a tape, that never materialized, with Michelle Obama allegedly referring to Caucasians as "whitey," and an allegation that Senator McCain was actually the cause of the explosion on the USS Forrestal in 1967 that claimed the lives of 134 sailors and that he only narrowly escaped, life intact, himself. Yet another call for news media investigation involving Senator McCain, alleged he engaged in behaving badly during a holiday trip to Fiji prior to his first run for the presidency, during which he supposedly insulted fellow vacationers and subjected them to his reading aloud from the works of William Faulkner. Though other tales of this nature were explained away as, proven to be untrue, about both candidates in the Politico story, one curious thing stood out about them all. With the exception of the USS Forrestal allegation against Senator McCain, the call for investigative reporting in regards to allegations against Senator Obama would have, arguably, done more damage to Obama's campaign for the presidency than any other allegation listed in the story about Senator McCain would have done to his efforts to win the General Election.

There was little doubt that the stories referred to as debunked regarding the two presidential contenders actually were a stretch of the imagination dreamed up by self interested parties seeking to derail one campaign or the other and to make it that much easier for the last man standing to claim the ultimate political prize. There was also little doubt that the allegations, referred to in the story, not investigated by the news media due to little or no evidence of validity, were dismissed legitimately. There was, however, validity to the assertion of the existence of a pattern of overt damage control efforts, on the part of the news media favoring one candidate over all others. There were hours upon hours and case upon case of proof of this. The latest effort by the *Los Angeles Times* to withhold video footage of an event, attended by Senator Obama, during which "nothing happened" seemed to only add to the mounting case against the American news media, citing bias and misconduct to facilitate an Obama General Election victory. If there was indeed nothing to see on the video, then there should have been no hesitation to release it to the McCain Campaign or other entities within the news media community for further inspection. After all, nothing from nothing leaves nothing. It did however seem hypocritical that the news media absolutely could not compromise the last shred of veracity left in its grasp, even after so many infractions of unbridled bias during the campaign season, to break a promise to an unnamed source not to leak the footage of the Khalidi video. Every nation should be so fortunate to have a news media with such integrity.

2 November 2008

As the closing argument of a political campaign that was as hard fought and long suffering as that of Senators John McCain and Barack Obama, the American news media, comfortable with Senator Obama's lead in the polls and engaging in low key recovery operations to salvage what was left of its image, saw fit to weigh in on the race one more time prior to the General Election. The final nail in the coffin of Senator McCain's campaign for the presidency would come in the form of an almost unanimous prediction by some of the news media's leading correspondents and political pundits regarding the outcome of the General Election of 2008. In a never before seen move, the news media placed itself in the position of final authority regarding the election, even ahead of the citizens of America yet to cast their votes. One by one, the correspondents and pundits submitted their predictions regarding the final tally of electoral votes, for release to news media outlets, in an effort to make known the Media Political Machine's choice for the presidency with a loud, thunderous, resounding, and unified voice. The verdict was the prediction of nothing less than a landslide victory of both mammoth and historic proportions in favor of freshman Senator Barack Obama of Illinois who was projected to put on a clinic for the veteran phoenix of the U.S. Senate, Senator John McCain of Arizona, teaching him the fundamentals of what it meant to be a winner. A partial list of the news media's predictions for the outcome of the 2008 General Election, posted on the AOL News Website, read as follows with regard to how these agents of the news media predicted the electoral vote chips would fall:

Chris Matthews, Correspondent MSNBC—*Obama* 338, McCain 200

Edward Rollins, Republican Campaign Consultant—*Obama* 353, McCain 185

Arianna Huffington, Editor-in-Chief, *The Huffington Post*—*Obama* 318, McCain 220

Fred Barns, Editor of the *Weekly Standard*—Obama 252, *McCain* 286

Donna Brazile, Democratic Strategist—*Obama* 343, McCain 195

George Will, Conservative Columnist—*Obama* 378, McCain 160

George Stephanopolous, ABC News host of "This Week"—*Obama* 353, McCain 185

Mark Halperin, *Time* magazine—*Obama* 349, McCain 189

David Gergen, CNN Political Analyst—*Obama* 338, McCain 200

Alex Castellanos, CNN Political Analyst and GOP media consultant—*Obama* 318, McCain 220

Eleanor Clift, *Newsweek* magazine Contributing Editor—*Obama* 349, McCain 189

So it was with the 2008 elections, during which much history was made in the course of roughly two years of the grueling and often times brutal campaign trail. Not soon to be a presidential race to be forgotten, American society and the world witnessed the first black nominee of a major American political party, the first former First Lady of the United States to ever run for the presidency, the first female to be nominated by the Republican Party to become Vice President of the United States, and the oldest person to ever be nominated for the presidency by a major American Political Party. The nation and the world also witnessed the emergence of an entity now known as the Media Political Machine that ran counter to enemy campaigns during the Democratic and Republican Party primaries as well as leading up to the General Election, lending unsolicited support to a campaign that was arguably light years ahead of even its most fierce competition in the eyes of American voters longing for change after a long, hard eight years under the reign of the second Bush Administration. After the dysfunctional and operationally challenged presidency of George W. Bush that ushered in a war on multiple fronts, a failing economy, and a shaky future for the once model nation for all others to follow, Senator Obama, with his message of change and hope, brought a yearning for tomorrow not seen in our mighty nation at least since the time of the Civil Rights Movement. Despite this reality, the American news media saw fit to attempt to force the hand of the people to do something that they were perhaps dead set on doing anyway. Only time would tell. Time would not, however erase the memory of the most negative campaign of the entire 2008 election season, bar none. The Media Political Machine comprised of all its toxic parts, including correspondents on the take, biased journalists, lopsided printed works, negative innuendoes, toxic props, negative lead ins, toxic broadcast specials, exaggerations, dramatics, star power, panel puppets, hype, demonizing, downplaying, leading questions, cover stories, pundits, mock subject matter experts, insinuation, and unsolicited damage control, ran a more negative campaign than perhaps any political party or candidate in our nation's entire history, and did so over the course of an almost two year period with progressive intensity relative to the proximity of the General Election. It further interfered with our nation's respected and envied democratic election process through the demolition of campaigns that ran counter to the news media's choice of who would be added to the annals of our free nation as the 44th President of the United States of America. Political cartoonist John Deering of the *Arkansas Democrat Gazette* captured the essence of what had occurred with a simple yet thought provoking depiction of the American news media's effects on the election that meant so much to an American society at its lowest point in decades. There was now little doubt that the Media Political Machine had made its position crystal clear. The conveyance of information ruled the nation, no matter what toxic form it came in.

Brazen and unchecked news media bias during the primaries and General Election of 2008 was as much a part of the history of perhaps the most important presidential election of our lifetime as the backgrounds of the candidates themselves with all the experience and substance each of them brought to the elections' political playing field. Early on in the election season, Walter Shorenstein, a California real estate developer, founder of the Joan Shorenstein Center on the Press, Politics and Public Policy at Harvard University, and loyal supporter of Hillary Clinton, expressed serious concern with bias on the part of the news media favoring Senator Obama and slamming Clinton particularly in regards to the effects it had on the Democratic primary election contests. In a memo to Democratic Party superdelegates and others critical of media coverage during the presidential campaign, Shorenstein wrote: "I am absolutely outraged with the media coverage of the presidential campaign. This is the most important election of my long lifetime, and to quote one of my favorite movies, 'I'm mad as hell and I'm not going to take it anymore!' Our democracy depends upon the fourth estate to fulfill the uniquely critical role of informing voters about the important issues facing our nation. Yet far too often, the campaign coverage has been biased, blasé, or baseless."[136]

Much later in the campaign season, regarding the toxic nature of the coverage of the '08 elections by the American news media, *Time* magazine's Mark Halperin, often hailed as one of the most respected political editors in America, expressed his disgust for the manner in which the press conducted itself, at a conference hosted by The Politico. Halperin concluded that the biased coverage was "the most disgusting failure of people in our business since the Iraq War."[137] Halperin further cited two irrefutable instances of pro-Obama media bias published during the election season committed by *The New York Times*.

> "The example that I use, at the end of the campaign, was the two profiles that The New York Times ran of the potential first ladies. The story about Cindy McCain was vicious. It looked for every negative thing they could find about her and it placed her in an extraordinarily negative light. It didn't talk about her work, for instance, as a mother for her

children, and they cherry- picked every negative thing that's ever been written about her.

The story about Michelle Obama, by contrast, was like a front-page endorsement of what a great person Michelle Obama is,"[138] Halperin concluded.

ABC political correspondent, Jake Tapper, agreed that media bias was apparent throughout the election and seemed to heavily favor Senator Obama. Tapper wrote in a blog regarding the occurrence:

Regular readers of this blog will not be surprised to learn that I too wonder how fair the media coverage of this campaign was.

Case in point: perhaps the most unfair and negative TV ad run during the entire campaign, by either side, was the Spanish-language TV ad Obama ran against Senator John McCain, R- Arizona, that got very little media coverage.

Why didn't it get more coverage? If McCain had run a comparable ad—with unfair charges, trying to exploit racial tensions—would it have been as under covered?

In any case, Obama won for any number of reasons, not the least of which were the modern Gold Standard in presidential campaigns and a nation that wanted dramatic change.

But I believe Halperin's larger point—since he brought in the media's rather wanting coverage of the build-up to the war in Iraq as well—is the fact that reporters have an obligation to be better.[139]

The Center for Media and Public Affairs also attested to heavy bias on the part of the news media favoring Senator Obama and frequently demonizing opposing candidates, after analyzing 979 separate news stories shown between August 23 and October 24 of 2008. Just as The Project for Excellence in Journalism concluded only a week earlier, Senator McCain received far more negative news coverage than Senator Obama in the days following the national party conventions. George Mason University professor and head of the Center for Media and Public Affairs, Robert Lichter stated, "For whatever reason, the media are portraying Barack Obama as a better choice for president than John McCain. If you watch the evening news, you'd think you should vote for Obama."[140]

Since the Pew Research Center for the People and the Press stated recently that it was its finding that cable television, particularly news networks, remains our nation's primary source for news regarding the elections, and since a significant percentage of cable news television viewers referred to themselves as yet undecided in regards to for whom they would vote almost up to the day of the General Election, there was no doubt that toxic and biased news media coverage of the 2008 campaign season had some manner of an effect on the outcome of the national election process. When coupled with the effects of our emotions on the decisions we make in the voting booth as explained by Drew Westen in his book *The Political Brain*,[141] the argument becomes even more compelling that the manner in which the American news media portrayed the candidates in 24 hour broadcasts and through lopsided publications, had a significant impact on some if not all of the elections in the race for the presidency in 2008. This being the case, the 2008 primaries and General Election marked the emergence of the American news media, aka the Media Political Machine, as a game changing political force with the potential to significantly impact or even determine the outcome of our nation's national elections in the future if left unchecked.

The most detrimental element of toxicity introduced into the 2008 presidential election was, without a doubt, the manner in which news media correspondents and journalists collectively attacked and destroyed the characters of candidates that found themselves outside of the Media Political Machine's favor. There was, seemingly, no end to how far agents of the news media were allowed to go, by their employing interests, to literally render several candidates unacceptable to American society to even be considered for the office of the presidency. Issues surrounding some of the candidates that were completely irrelevant to the primaries and General Election were repeatedly brought to the forefront of round the clock news media coverage and magnified in a manner that made at least two of the candidates seem to be the embodiment of all the characteristics of the anti-Christ. This from self righteous news media agents that, in most cases, had scarcely a fraction of the education, experience, and integrity of the candidates and those associated with the campaigns of which they were so critical and campaigned so steadfastly and consistently against. The question then lingered in the heads of all concerned persons that witnessed this travesty, how could these demon candidates have slipped through the cracks of our political system to rise to such prominence to even be considered for the American presidency if they were indeed the quintessence of all things bad? The answer to this is simple. Those subject to the ruthlessness of the self interest driven American news media during the 2008 presidential election race were no better or worse than any politician that has ever walked the halls of our nation's most prominent political institutions. The news media only made them seem that way to feed its ever growing appetite for money, power, influence, and notoriety for history making and groundbreaking coverage of a page turning event in our nation's history. Moreover, it did not matter to them that they may have helped to force the page's turning. Maybe now, the boldest of these is saying, "So what?!"

Here is what. In a 1966 episode of the once popular western television series, "The Big Valley," titled "Target," a candidate for the office of governor accused the Barkleys, the show's wealthy, benevolent, and reputable lead role family of gaining their wealth through less than honorable means. After a night of heavy drinking, the politician knocked over a lit kerosene lamp in his hotel room then slipped into a drunken stupor on a nearby couch. When a friend, staying the night in an adjoining hotel room, smelled smoke, he broke into the candidate's room to put the fire out. After the fire was extinguished by the friend, the candidate awoke to the sight of a crowd gathered at his door as a result of the commotion. The candidate then quickly sobered up, and like a true politician, took the opportunity to address the crowd, now attendees of a hasty political rally. During his impromptu address, he made several more unflattering accusations against the Barkley family, even going as far as stating that associates of the family started the fire in his room in an effort to kill him. Though the Barkley family was known in the town to be a hardworking, reputable, and noble pillar of their community, when the publisher of the "reputable" town newspaper heard about the slanderous accusation made against the Barkleys by the gubernatorial candidate, he took advantage of the controversy to sell more copies of the publication by printing the story on the paper's front page. Simply due to the fact the town newspaper, as a trusted source for newsworthy and factual information, chose to publish the scandal, many townspeople who read the story took the accusations of fraud and attempted murder leveled against the Barkley family to be factual. Though the publisher's purpose for printing the story was self-serving, superficial, and shallow in nature, bringing him only a temporary monetary gain at best, the damage to the reputation of the Barkley family as a result of the accusations, that were all later proven to be completely false, would have, no doubt had a long lasting effect.

Much like the fictitious Barkley family in the 1966 episode of "The Big Valley," many candidates involved in the race for the presidency in 2008 were subject to this extreme manner of slander and demonizing that had a noticeably detrimental effect on both their character and their campaigns. The only difference was that instead of the toxicity originating from opposing campaigns or candidates, the lion's share of slanderous, character assassinating attacks originated in the studios and at the presses of the American news media. The same news media once charged with keeping our nation's citizens well informed regarding factual and newsworthy occurrences on a local, national, and global level, effecting their everyday lives, had betrayed the trust of the American people in efforts to influence the outcome of the most important elections that many of them would ever see during the course of their lifetimes. What was worse, was the fact that since the conveyance of toxic information in its most biased and slanderous form went unchecked, future political candidates and American voters would undoubtedly be subjected to the wrath of the Media Political Machine during future national campaigns and elections. The continued tolerance of this activity will successfully take the power of our democracy out of the hands of its citizens and place it firmly in the hands of the controlling interests of the news media that could make or break political candidates with the publishing of a doting article or by repeatedly uttering defamatory remarks and innuendos about them.

At the same time some candidates suffered a fate similar to "The Big Valley's" Barkley family, finding themselves combating the news media's unabashed bias against them, another candidate enjoyed a celebrity status with the press never before seen by the citizens of this nation, catapulting him from the status of Washington political newcomer, to "rock star," almost overnight. Senator Barack Obama, from the earliest days of the primary elections of 2008 up to the final days of the General Election campaigns, was the recipient of an undeniably unprecedented amount of favorable coverage on the part of the news media that amounted to free advertisement for a candidate that was already strategically light years ahead of even his closest competitors and had a campaign contribution war chest totaling around three quarters of a billion dollars by the end of the '08 election season. In a poll conducted by Rasmussen Reports, a public opinion polling firm founded by pollster Scott Rasmussen, co-founder of ESPN, Rasmussen determined that 49% of the nation's population believed most agents of the news media were indeed trying to aid Senator Obama in ultimately winning the 2008 General Election. While the media's love affair with Senator Obama was both unsolicited and unwarranted, the media consistently portrayed him as almost perfect at the same time it shamelessly magnified the slip ups and shortcomings of his fiercest rivals. This essentially rendered his already immaculate image that much more appealing to the fence sitters, the undecided, and the uncertain voters in our society. PR services extended to Senator Obama by the Media Political Machine, free of charge, while it was denied to all other candidates during the 2008 elections, included an astronomical amount of favorable front page coverage, favorable coverage clarifying and defending his campaign platforms, as well as news media damage control during the most challenging controversies. It should also be noted that Senator Obama, no doubt, holds the record for the most times a person's name was said during a single news media broadcast.

The unfortunate thing about the entire affair, was the fact that with the team of political masterminds, the number of campaign donors and loyal supporters, and the throngs of American citizens seeking change after the dark ages ushered in by the Bush

Administration, Senator Obama would have most likely emerged victorious on the night of the General Election anyway, and likely by a significant margin. Whatever the percentage of the margin of advantage that was facilitated by the overt bias of the news media, no matter how miniscule, should however be resolutely denounced by all our nation's citizens because the blatant unfairness of it goes against all things democratic. The shameful acts committed by the pillars of the American news media during the 2008 elections, further, should not be simply written off as something that "just happened" and that those most concerned about its occurrence should just "get over," as several partisans have suggested regarding the mistakes and no-calls made leading up to the invasion of Iraq. Standing silently and idly by concerning this mockery would mean approving the authorization for the rogue American news media mob to commit these acts, detrimental to the veracity of our democracy, again and again until they have wrestled all power from the hands of the people, and eventually our national government through biased coverage that stirs the emotions of the masses—for better or worse. If the news media can influence image, it can influence opinion, if it can influence opinion, it can influence the vote, if it can influence the vote, it can influence the outcome, if it can influence the outcome, it will then attempt to influence the victor, and so on. The question then becomes where will it stop? As evidenced by the incidents of sustained overt and unapologetic news media bias and toxicity during the 2008 elections even after the media was repeatedly made aware of the nation's citizens' displeasure with the toxic and lopsided coverage, the answer is *it will not.*

As with anything, there were many naysayers, and those that could not see the forest for the trees, that denied the presence of widespread and unimpeded bias on the part of the news media during the 2008 election season. The individuals that steadfastly supported the argument that little if any bias was present during coverage of the elections and campaigns fit into one of three categories. The first category is for those that simply did not tune in to or read much of what the Media Political Machine was selling regarding the candidates and their campaigns, and that perhaps obtained most information regarding the elections on a local level such as from city or state circulated newspapers outside of the political arm of the

Media Political Machine's realm of influence. The second category of naysayers belongs to those that believe everything they hear on television and everything they read in print simply because it is on television or in print. These people had no reason to question the information put out by the news media regarding the elections, because by virtue of the news media conveying the information on live broadcasts or printing it in nationally circulated magazines or newspapers, in their minds, it was rendered factually sound and objective. The final category of those that denied the presence of news media bias during the '08 election season belongs to those that refused to admit to the presence of the toxicity and lopsidedness of the news media's coverage because it benefited the candidate or candidates they supported. For these people, it did not matter that a flag should have been thrown on the several plays of the ball game. What mattered to them most was their team was winning.

The most commonly asked questions of those that argued the media provided balanced news coverage during the course of the election season, often found in news media publications and in entries from bloggers debating the subject were, one, where is the proof of media bias during the elections, and two, what would the news media stand to gain from providing round the clock biased coverage of the candidates and their campaigns? While the proof of the pudding regarding the many ways the American news media injected bias and toxicity into coverage of the 2008 elections can easily be found between the pages of this book, and arguments to support this claim have been issued by some of the most prominent names in American news media circles, the question of what the media would stand to gain does warrant a more detailed analysis. For those that denied the presence of toxicity and bias during the news media's coverage of the '08 elections based upon the argument that the news industry would have nothing to gain from doing so, I present the following three arguments for consideration in the spirit of motive.

In the American news media world, careers are made, aside from simply being good at what one does, by the accumulation of experience covering newsworthy events. The most notable of these events covered often go into a given agent of the news media's biography which provides credibility for his or her capability to cover more newsworthy events in an effective and competent manner. While news media correspondents and journalists are many times found to be light in the education department, though they, at times, portray themselves as experts in all things, their profession affords them the opportunity to make up for this shortfall through experience. In biographies of news media correspondents and journalists, phrases attesting to a news media agent's coverage experience are heavily relied upon to round out a resume. Examples of these include, X "traveled with Cheney to the Middle East in 2002 as the administration began to build support for confronting Saddam Hussein." Another example of this is, "The 2008 campaign is the sixth presidential election he has covered." Unfortunately, many news media entities have come to believe that experience covering such events renders a person a subject matter expert in that particular area. In any case, the coverage of such events by a given journalist or correspondent, in the world of news media, contributes significantly to his or her reputation as a serious agent of the American news media.

In addition to gaining credibility from merely covering or reporting on newsworthy events, this credibility is multiplied by the significance or magnitude of the event covered. For example, a journalist or correspondent, employed by a major news media entity, that covered the events in the aftermath of Hurricane Katrina could be regarded as more experienced than one that only had experience covering events of a much less significant or prominent nature. This being true, it is not hard to see that if a given correspondent or journalist provided coverage throughout the hotly contested primaries and General Election of 2008, and the outcome yielded the nation's first black president, these parties would have much to gain in the way of credibility and notoriety in news media circles from that day forward. The line in their biographies would then read, "X was this network's primary political correspondent during the 2008 presidential elections and the election of the first black President of the United States." A historically significant event of this nature could easily become the crowning achievement in the career of a leading correspondent or journalist therefore providing a clear motive for facilitating such an election outcome through conveying newsworthy facts in an unfair, unbalanced, and un-objective manner.

In addition to individual correspondents, journalists, and other agents of the news media standing to gain much by supporting a win for Senator Barack Obama on November 4, 2008, the news media industry, as a collective, also had a clear motive for providing heavily biased news coverage in his favor during the election season. Since the launch of the Internet, many arms of the American news media, mainly those circulated in printed form, have experienced a steady decline in sales and advertising revenue, leading to downsizing and regular layoffs. When it began to seem that an African American newcomer to the national political scene actually had a shot at winning both the Democratic Party nomination as well as the General Election, it was realized that this was exactly the type of earth shattering story that the news media had been waiting for. Not only would it provide the much needed shot of adrenaline that the print media had been looking for to boost its sales of publications that, time and time again undersold at the newsstand, but it would also allow the news media to heavily influence the outcome of the election through what it chose to and not to print based on a demand that it, in part, helped to create. A statement made around the time of the 2008 national elections by Janice Min, Chief Editor of *US Weekly*, pointed to the former as a possible hidden agenda on the part of the news media during the elections. Min stated, regarding the Barack Obama story in general, that it was, "something the print industry has been dying to come along."[142] This being the case, it is not so farfetched to assert the news media was not above glamorizing, embellishing upon, and churching up the story of a man who, though iconic in his own right, upon being elected as the country's 44th President, could bring about the greatest demand for news media publications since September 11—and for much longer.

Adding to the star power and gravitas of Senator Barack Obama's image during the '08 elections through overwhelmingly favorable news media coverage brought to fruition two things of significance for the American news media. The first of these was an increase in revenue, generated by a news media facilitated demand for publications featuring Senator Obama that could be prematurely marketed as collector's items, due to the historic nature and significance of the *possibility* of the election of the first nonwhite President in the nation's history. The second of these would be, upon Senator Obama actually being elected as the next President of the United States, another increase in revenue fueled by the sales of the first copies of print media publications featuring him as the nation's first African American President, followed closely by pricey commemorative edition reprints and bookazine's, recounting the days leading up to one of the most significant and historical events to occur in the history of our nation. In addition to this, the news media would also have the opportunity to stretch out the public's interest in Obama by marketing every publication and broadcast using his iconic image and providing up to the minute coverage of every single first that Obama would ever do as the nation's "first African American President." Among these would be the inauguration of the nation's first black President, the first piece of legislation signed into law by the nation's first black President, the first time a black President steps off of Air Force One, the first ever press conference held by the nation's first black President and so on. The American news media could potentially milk this process for years to come until it squeezed every drop of revenue out of the sale of Obama's image and his historical significance which is another clear motive for covering the elections in a manner that favored him and was far less kind to others.

Finally, the most threatening motive for the news media's display of blatant bias during the 2008 elections is the Media Political Machine's desire to control the outcome of this and future General Elections through the conveyance of toxic and heavily biased information directly impacting the view the nation's citizens have of the candidates involved in our democratic election process. By employing the tactics of a seemingly ever growing arsenal of very influential and ill intended communications techniques to inject toxicity into information about candidates and campaigns associated with national elections, the American news media launched a successful all out assault on the foundation of the world's strongest and most revered democracy. By actively engaging in a clandestine campaign to put a drag on and derail the campaigns of several of the '08 campaign season's top candidates, and succeeding at doing so, as evidenced repeatedly throughout the elections, the news media freely exercised a power and authority over the election process never before witnessed by the nation's citizens. The uninhibited audacity that the most prominent agents and organizations within the news media community displayed while openly campaigning for and against candidates and their campaigns in round the clock venues during the '08 elections, reflected the determination of a once trustworthy pillar of this society to wrestle the reins from the hands of the people and exercise supreme authority over our nation's national election process. The successful establishment of the Media Political Machine during such an important time in our nation's political history also served as the ultimate test for the nation's news media which betrayed the trust of the nation's citizens and took advantage of their tired and weakened state after almost eight years of a broken executive branch of government, a seemingly endless multi-front war, and an ever worsening economic situation.

In regards to this motive for the news media's toxic coverage of the '08 elections, the benefit yielded from its undertaking would be two fold. The first benefit to the American news media would be the power to dictate to the nation's citizens, using both overt and covert tactics in regular broadcasts and nationally circulated publications, who the nation's next President would be. If the news media succeeded in exercising significant influence over the voting populace to accomplish this, the door would be wide open for the Media Political Machine to exercise the same form of influence in future elections, employing the same tactics used to damage the images and reputation of candidates of its choosing while blatantly covering others in a far more favorable manner. Further, if the news media is allowed to continue to exercise this form of control over the democratic process of our national elections, it will mark the beginning of the end of the last shreds of power held by the American voter in regards to the same.

The second benefit of this motive behind the news media's unfettered and brazenly apparent bias during the '08 elections would be the implications a successful clandestine national political campaign would mean for the Media Political Machine. A successful hostile takeover of the national election process through openly campaigning in favor of or trashing candidates and their campaigns would mean that eventually the news media will seek to advance its sphere of influence and exercise some form of control over the victors of national elections, using air waves and publications to either support or criticize him or her as a unified political voice. The result of this could mean that a nationally elected official would be pressured or swayed by the news media's negative coverage and spin of important issues and decisions to be made by that official. An example of this would be the news media providing highly negative coverage in regards to a person a President-Elect is considering to serve as the nation's next Secretary of State in hopes that he will bend to the news media's sentiments and select another individual to fill the post.[143] The first time our nation's elected leaders cave to this form of pressure from the American news media will decisively mark the end of democracy as we know it and the beginning of the undisputed reign of the Media Political Machine.

On Tuesday, November 4, 2008, I hastily made my way to the small city in Central Arkansas, that I call home, to cast what was perhaps the most important vote in a national election of my entire life. It was morning and the polling station was just opening, as I wanted to cast my vote early enough so as not encounter any issues that I had heard about being endured by some early voters. As I pulled off the interstate and onto the highway leading into town, I thought about every broadcast I viewed and publication that I had read regarding the last candidates standing in the doorway to the Oval Office. As I passed through each traffic light, I compared the credentials of the two candidates that I had gained greater insight into both from my own research efforts as well as from the toxic coverage that the news media industry provided over roughly a two year period. I turned into the parking lot of my polling place, the old county courthouse, just as the first voters were coming out the doors with tiny slips of paper in their hands indicating that they had completed the all important undertaking that I too would accomplish along with millions of American voters that day. I felt a little uneasy as I entered the double doors and walked down the dark, dimly lit hallway, following the signs down to the basement where the voting machines were set up. I saw many familiar faces when I finally made it into the small chamber below. They smiled and spoke as they passed, but I was too preoccupied with my own thoughts about the election to even comprehend what any of them said. I gave my identification card to one of the nice elderly ladies at the table set up for registration and signed my name in the district election books for the thirteenth time in my adult life. I then turned about and walked into the tiny room with only four machines set up to log and tally votes. The election official in the room promptly directed me to an open machine and started the touch screen login process, getting me to the election start page. When I finally made it through the gauntlet of lesser elections and proposed state legislation items, I came to a page that allowed for me, a small town American citizen of this great nation, to cast my vote for the 44th President of the United States of America, and the next leader of the free world. Though there were several candidates listed, there were only two candidates that I chose from for which to vote, Senator John McCain of Arizona and Senator Barack Obama of Illinois. At this point my mind was made, and I nervously touched the icon beside the name of none other than Senator Barack Obama, feeling that he was indeed the right man at the right time to lead our nation at such a challenging period in its history. I left my polling station that day feeling confident that I had made the right decision and one that was in the best interest of our nation. Despite this heartfelt sentiment, however, I could not shake the feeling that the Media Political Machine had, in some manner, helped me to arrive at my conclusion.

NOTES AND SOURCES

[1]   Alan Duke, Steve Brusk, Mike Roselli, CNN, "Clinton says she 'misspoke' about sniper fire," [http://www.cnn.com/2008/POLITICS/03/25/campaign.wrap/index.html], March 2008.

[2]   Ibid.

[3]   Ibid.

[4]   Reference material spinelessly removed from MSNBC Website and the World Wide Web

[5]   Eleanor Clift, *Newsweek*, "Why Clinton is Fighting So Hard: If Obama wins, Clinton's own legacy looks smaller by comparison," [http://www.newsweek.com/id/131524], April 2008.

[6]   Ibid.

[7]   Ibid.

[8]   Ibid.

[9]   CNN, Anderson Cooper 360 Degrees Hosted by John King, [http://transcripts.cnn.com/TRANSCRIPTS/0804/25/acd.01.html], April 2008.

[10]   Ibid.

[11]   Ibid.

[12]   Ibid.

[13]   Ibid.

14   Hardball with Chris Matthews, [http://www.msnbc.msn.com/id/24369356/print/1/displaymode/1098/], April 2008.

15   Ibid.

16   CNN, Larry King Live, Michael Moore on the 2008 Election, [http://transcripts.cnn.com/TRANSCRIPTS/0804/30/lkl.01.html], April 2008.

17   Ibid.

18   Ibid.

19   David Kiley, "Clinton Decidedly Negative A Day Before the New Super Tuesday," [http://www.businessweek.com/the_thread/brandnewday/archives/2008/03/Clinton_goes_de.html], March 2003.

20   Roland Martin, CNN, "Commentary: Forget an Obama-Clinton or Clinton-Obama ticket," [http://www.cnn.com/2008/POLITICS/02/04/roland.martin/index.html], February 2008.

21   Ibid.

22   Libby Quaid, Associated Press, "McCain's temper may prove to be a liability," [http://www.usatoday.com/news/politics/election2008/2008-02-17-mccain-temper_N.htm], February 2008.

23   Jon Meacham and Evan Thomas, "Mr. Cool vs. Mr. Hot: The Vices of Their Virtues," *Newsweek*, 6 October, 2008, 22-23.

24   Dana Bash, Peter Hamby, John King, with contribution by Ed Hornick, CNN, "Palin's 'going rogue,' McCain aide says," [http://www.cnn.com/2008/POLITICS/10/25/palin.tension/], October 2008.

25   Joan Morgan, *Vibe Magazine*, "Don't Call It A Comeback," [http://www.vibe.com/news/online_exclusives/2008/02/decision08_hillary_clinton_obama/], February 2008.

26   CNN, The Situation Room Hosted by Wolf Blitzer, [http://transcripts.cnn.com/TRANSCRIPTS/0805/06/sitroom.02html], May 2008.

27   Ibid.

28   Ibid.

29   BrandingIron, NowPublic, "Media Bias Against Clinton and What Obama Doesn't Want You to Know," [http://www.nowpublic.com/world/media-bias-against-clinton-and-what-obama-doesn't-want-you-know]

30   "And the Winner* Is…," *Time* magazine, Volume 171, Number 20, May 2008.

31   CNN Anderson Cooper 360 Degrees, [http://transcripts.cnn.com/TRANSCRIPTS/0805/13/acd.02.html], May 2008.

32   CNN, Special Investigations Unit Hosted by Dr. Sanjay Gupta, "The First Patient: Health and the Presidency," [http://transcripts.cnn.com/TRANSCRIPTS/0806/02/acd.02.html], May 2008.

33   Todd Purdum, *Vanity Fair*, "The Comeback Id," [http://www.vanityfair.com/politics/features/2008/07/clinton200807], July 2008.

34   Ibid.

35   CNN Anderson Cooper 360 Degrees, [http://transcripts.cnn.com/TRANSCRIPTS/0806/02/acd.02.html], June 2008.

36   Joe Klein, *Time* Magazine, "Can Hillary Unite the Party?" [http://www/time.com/time/politics/article/0,8599,1811832,00.html], June 2008.

37   Ibid.

38   Ibid.

39   Ibid.

40   Ibid.

41   Alex Daniels, "Clinton Calls It Quits, Puts Her Bid On Ice," *Arkansas Democrat Gazette*, 8 June, 2008.

42   Ibid.

43   CNN, Your Money, Your Vote Hosted by Campbell Brown, [http://transcripts.cnn.com/TRANSCRIPTS/0806/09/acd.02.html], June 2008.

44   Ibid.

45   *Huffington Post*, "Keith Olbermann Names Katie Couric 'Worst Person In the World'," [http://www.huffingtonpost.com/2008/06/12/keith-olbermann-names-kat_n_106689.html], June 2008.

46   CNN American Morning, [http://transcripts.cnn.com/TRANSCRIPTS/0806/27/ltm.03.html], June 2008.

47   Ibid.

48   Ibid.

49   The Associated Press, *New York Daily News*, "Clark Comments on McCain Military Service," [http://www.nydailynews.com/

news/politics/2008/06/30/2008-06-30_wesley_clark_john_mccain_lacks_command_e.html], June 2008.

50   Douglas Valentine, *Counterpunch*, "John McCain: War Hero or North Vietnam's Go-To Collaborator?" [http://www.counterpunch.org/valentine06132008.html], June 2008.

51   Ibid.

52   CNN Larry King Live, Hosted by Glenn Beck, [http://transcripts.cnn.com/TRANSCRIPTS/0807/21/lkl.01.html], July 2008.

53   Ibid.

54   Jodi Kantor, *The New York Times*, "Teaching Law, Testing Ideas, Obama Stood Slightly Apart," [http://www.nytimes.com/2008/07/30/us/politics/30law.html], July 2008.

55   CNN Election Center, [http://transcripts.cnn.com/TRANSCRIPTS/0808/04/ec.01.html], August 2008.

56   Ibid.

57   CNN Anderson Cooper 360 Degrees, [http://transcripts/cnn.com/TRANSCRIPTS/0808/07.acd.01.html], August 2008.

58   Joshua Green, "The Front-Runner's Fall," *The Atlantic*, Volume 302, Number 2, September 2008, 64-74.

59   Ibid, pg. 68.

60   James Carville, *Stickin': The Case for Loyalty*, (Simon and Schuster, 2000).

61   CNN The Situation Room, [http://transcripts.cnn.com/TRANSCRIPTS/0804/09/sitroom.03.html], April 2008.

62   CNN Politics.com, [http://www.cnn.com/2008/POLITICS/05/26/veepstakes/], June 2008.

63   Ibid.

64   Reference material spinelessly removed by CNN due to the toxic content of the narrative smearing Senator Hillary Clinton during election season 2008. The Pro/Con format for the Democratic VP hopefuls was changed to a version that was far less offensive and biased against Clinton. [http://www.cnn.com/2008/POLITICS/06/03/possible.dems.vps/index.html], June 2008.

65   Reference material spinelessly removed by CNN due to the toxic content of the narrative smearing Senator Hillary Clinton during election season 2008. The Pro/Con format for the Democratic VP hopefuls was changed to a version that was

far less offensive and biased against Clinton. [http://www.cnn.com/2008/POLITICS/06/03/possible.dems.vps/index.html], June 2008.

66   CNN   Politics.com,   [http://www.cnn.com/2008/POLITICS/05/26/veepstakes/], June 2008.

67   *Huffington Post,* Jack Cafferty: "If Sarah Palin Being One Heartbeat Away Doesn't Scare The Hell Out Of You, It Should," [http://www.huffingtonpost.com/2008/09/26/jack-cafferty-if-sarah-pa_n_129724.html], September 2008.

68   CBSNews.com, "Alaska National Guard Hit 'Crisis Level,'" [http://www.cbsnews.com/stories/2008/09/04/national/main4414482.shtml], September 2008.

69   Ibid.

70   CBSNews.com, "Sarah Palin Delivers Smash Hit In St. Paul," [http://www.cbsnews.com/stories/2008/09/04/politics/main4413965.shtml], September 2008.

71   Ibid.

72   Ibid.

73   CBSNews.com, Story spinelessly removed from the CBS News Website, however, Ververs quote also found in another CBS News story titled: "Obama Accuses McCain of 'Phony Outrage,'" [http://www.cbsnews.com/stories/2008/09/10/politics/main4434087.shtml], September 2008.

74   Larry Rohter, *The New York Times,* "Ad On Sex Education Distorts Obama Policy," [http://www.nytimes.com/2008/09/11/us/politics/11checkpoint.html], September 2008.

75   Ibid.

76   KimberlyKindy, *Washington Post,* "A Tangled Story of Addiction," [http://www.washingtonpost.com/wp-dyn/content/article/2008/09/11/AR2008091103928.html], September 2008.

77   Ibid.

78   Ibid.

79   Ibid.

80   MSNBC, MSNBC Transcripts, [http://www.msnbc.msn.com/id/26841793/], September 2008.

81   Hannah Strange, *Times Online,* "Palin Linked Electoral Success to Prayer of Kenyan Witchhunter," [http://timesonline.typepad.

com/uselections/2008/09/palin-linked-el.html],   September 2008.

82   MSNBC, MSNBC Transcripts, [http://www.msnbc.msn.com/id/26841793/], September 2008.

83   Jonathan Mahler, *Newsweek*, "The Ur-Text of a Tabloid Age," [http://www.newsweek.com/id/160082], September 2008.

84   Ibid.

85   Journalism.org, Pew Research Center's Project for Excellence in Journalism, "The Color of News: Cable—Three Different Networks, Three Different Perspectives," [http://www.journalism.org/node/13436], October 2008.

86   Ibid.

87   Jonathan Mahler, *Newsweek*, "The Ur-Text of a Tabloid Age," [http://www.newsweek.com/id/160082], September 2008.

88   Brian Montopoli, CBSNews.com, "NRA Begins Push to Tarnish Obama On Guns," [http://www/cbsnews.com/stories/2008/09/23/politics/main4472798.shtml],   September 2008.

89   Ibid.

90   Ibid.

91   Democrat-Gazette Press Services, "1ˢᵗ Debate: Both Claim They Won," *Arkansas Democrat Gazette*, 28 September 2008.

92   Ibid.

93   Ibid.

94   Ibid.

95   CNN, Fareed Zakaria GPS, [http://transcripts.cnn.com/TRANSCRIPTS/0809/28/fzgps.01.html], September 2008.

96   Jon Meacham and Evan Thomas, "The Vices of Their Virtues," *Newsweek*, 6 October, 2008, 22-23.

97   Ibid.

98   Ibid.

99   Ibid.

100   Ibid.

101   Ibid.

102   Ibid.

103   Ibid.

104   CNN, CNN Live Events Special, "Dissecting the Vice Presidential Candidate's Debate," [http://edition.cnn.hu/TRANSCRIPTS/0810/04/se.02.html], October 2008.

105   CNN, CNN Presents, "Fit To Lead: An Historical Overview of the Health Concerns, And Medical Care Of The U.S. Presidency," [http://transcripts.cnn.com/TRANSCRIPTS/0810/11/cp.01.html], October 2008.

106   Ibid.

107   Editorial, *The New York Times*, "Politics of Attack," [http://www.nytimes.com/2008/10/08/opinion/08wed1.html], October 2008.

108   CNN, CNN Political Ticker, "New York Times Calls McCain Campaign 'Appalling'," [http://politicalticker.blogs.cnn.com/category/new-york-times/], October 2008.

109   Ibid.

110   Jon Meacham, "The Palin Problem," *Newsweek*, 13 October, 2008, 40-44.

111   CNN, CNN Presents, "Fit To Lead: An Historical Overview of the Health Concerns, And Medical Care Of The U.S. Presidency," [http://transcripts.cnn.com/TRANSCRIPTS/0810/11/cp.01.html], October 2008.

112   Ibid.

113   Eric Deggans, "Love At First Sight," *Newsmax*, October 2008, 56-64.

114   Ibid.

115   Ibid.

116   MSNBC, "Powell Endorses Obama for President: Republican Ex-Secretary of State Calls Democrat 'Transformational Figure'," [http://www.msnbc.msn.com/id/27265369/], October 2008.

117   CNN, CNN Political Ticker, "Three Major Papers Endorsed Obama," [http://politicalticker.blogs.cnn.com/2008/10/17/obama-wins-backing-from-three-major-metropolitan-newspapers/], October 2008.

118   CNN Transcript unavailable.

119   CBSNews.com, "Obama Rallies Supporters In Colorado," [http://www.cbsnews.com/stories/2008/10/26/politics/main4546330.shtml], October 2008.

[120] CBSNews.com, "McCain: 1/3 Palin Clothes Already Returned," [http://www.cbsnews.com/stories/2008/10/26/politics/main4546247.shtml], October 2008.

[121] CBSNews.com, "Obama Rallies Supporters In Colorado," [http://www.cbsnews.com/stories/2008/10/26/politics/main4546330.shtml], October 2008.

[122] Ibid.

[123] CBSNews.com, "McCain: 1/3 Palin Clothes Already Returned," [http://www.cbsnews.com/stories/2008/10/26/politics/main4546247.shtml], October 2008.

[124] LATimes.com, "New Mexico Newspaper Headline: Obama Wins!", [http://latimesblogs.latimes.com/thedishrag/2008/10/new-mexico-news.html], October 2008.

[125] John F. Harris and Jim Vandehei, "Why McCain Is Getting Hosed in the Press," Politico.com, [http://www.politico.com/news/stories/1008/14982.html], October 2008.

[126] Ibid.

[127] Ibid.

[128] Ibid.

[129] Ibid.

[130] Ibid.

[131] Ibid.

[132] Ibid.

[133] Ben Smith, "Cover This! Inside the Nastiest '08 Rumors," Politico.com, [http://www.politico.com/news/stories/1008/15106.html], October 2008.

[134] Ibid.

[135] Ibid.

[136] Walter Shorenstein, "Persistent Media Bias in Favor of Barack Obama and Against Hillary Clinton," [http://marcambinder.theatlantic.com/Important%20memo%20from%20Walter%20Shorenstein%20on%20Press%20and%20the%20Presidential%20Campaign.pdf], October 2008.

[137] Alexander Burns, "TIME's Mark Halperin,: 'Extreme Obama Bias a Disgusting Failure," *The Huffington Post,* [http://www.huffingtonpost.com/2008/11/22/times-mark-halperin-extre_n_145755.html], July 2008.

[138] Ibid.

139   Jake Tapper, "Halperin Decries 'Disgusting' Pro-Obama Media Bias In Election Coverage," ABC News, [http://blogs.abcnews.com/politicalpunch/2008/11/halperin-decrie.html], November 2008.

140   Post by Vaghn Ververs, "Study: Media Coverage Has Favored Obama," [http://www.cbsnews.com/sections/politics/horserace/main502163.shtml?start=80&90], November 2008.

141   Drew Westen, *The Political Brain: The Role of Emotion in Deciding the Fate of the Nation*, (Public Affairs, 2007).

142   Johnnie L. Roberts, *Newsweek*, "Can Obama Save the Media?" [http://www.newsweek.com/id/168933], November 2008.

143   Ken Silverstein, *Harper's*, "Hillary Clinton Should Not Be SecretaryofState,"[http://www.huffingtonpost.com/2008/11/17/ken-silverstein-five-reas_n_144365.html], November 2008.

HELP ME TO STAMP OUT TOXIC NEWS REPORTING TACTICS, KEEPING IT FREE FROM UNECCESSARY BIAS AND BULL. FOLLOW ME AT: http://twitter.com/Whosinthetank BEGINNING 1 OCTOBER 2009.